THE WORLD BELOW

David Peak

The World Below

ISBN-13: 978-1-954899-00-1
ISBN-10: 1-954899-00-9

Cover design by George Cotronis

www.apocalypse-party.com

First Edition

Printed in the U.S.A

There is no other world. Nor even this one. What, then, is there?

–Cioran

LETITIA UNDERHILL, 1999

Two things borne of one are forever connected. They complete each other. A baby and its mama are bonded by blood. The stars in the nighttime sky shine only because they swim in darkness. And no one knows what's good in the world unless they've glimpsed the eyes of evil.

It's like how things in the natural world coil into themselves and find an inner strength. You can't ever separate what belongs together, not when they're parts of a whole. Even when a piece of something looks like it's missing, it's still there—you just can't see it. The crescent moon is still the full moon, only part of it is secreted away, waiting to be revealed.

They say the Moon was formed after a chunk of rock as big as Mars came hurtling from the depths of outer space and smashed into Earth. This was billions of years ago, of course, long before man ever stood on two legs and declared himself master of the universe.

Two celestial bodies locked in a dance until the end of time, the snake eating its own tail, spinning round and round. Scientists named the rock that crashed into the Earth after the Greek goddess

Theia, daughter of Gaia, who then gave birth to Selene, goddess of the Moon.

How fitting was that? A mother and her daughter, an act of irreparable violence, the baby ripped free of the womb—two things borne of one.

For a fleeting moment, Lettie's world trembled. She wiped her tears away without thought. She couldn't think about her mother right now. Not now, not ever. Some feelings just opened up into an abyss.

It helped to focus on what was beautiful. There was always beauty to be found, often quiet and unassuming. The world ached with it. And for Lettie, beauty was a source of strength. She knew she was young. She knew she was beautiful. And she knew that these two things—her youth and her beauty—gave her power over boys and men alike.

She sat on the cushioned window bench in her bedroom, knees tucked to her chest, taking deep pulls on a hand-rolled cigarette. Pink Floyd's *The Piper at the Gates of Dawn* played softly on the stereo.

It was the middle of June and the school year was nearly over. The humid night was charged with heat. Fat, frail moths crashed dumbly against the ceiling, fluttering against the light. Her family's old house didn't have air conditioning, the rotting window swollen and stubborn on sweltering nights like these, the occasional gust of sweet summer air caressing the trees in the yard below.

Lettie was tired of waiting. She tossed the cigarette, went to the minifridge near her bed, and got the shrink-wrapped package of frozen feeder mice. Each little pinkie looked creased like a severed finger, their chilled flesh oddly bloodless. She removed the lid of her ball python's terrarium and dropped in one of the faceless little things.

Coiled beneath the large plastic log, Syd made no immediate movements. Feeding, hunger, those were just part of the cycle of life. Snakes had to eat just like everything else. One creature needs to feed on another to survive, to grow stronger, the cycle spinning round and round.

She gently stroked the snake's flat head with her finger. There, now. Syd flicked her red forked tongue. There was an understanding between animals and humans, but only where skin met skin. Some languages were older and more powerful than words.

Lettie returned to the window bench. A short while later she saw the orange flame of a Zippo lighter at the edge of the yard. The flame held constant for five seconds before it was snuffed out. Another five seconds passed before it returned. Orn was out there, waiting for her. Her heart pounded. Lettie grabbed the duffel bag from under her bed, already packed and ready to go, and tossed it out the window. She followed after it, quietly dropping onto the roof of the porch, making her way down the vine-tangled garden trellis. The moment her feet touched the ground she grabbed the bag and ran.

She met Orn beneath an old tree. He wore the same beat-up trucker hat as always, its frayed brim painstakingly curved. He took her hand in his and helped her over the fence. The smell of him was entirely his own, both familiar and strange, wood spice, open fields and moonlight. He smelled like freedom.

The whole world looked dusted with diamonds. Radiant blue cosmic clouds shifted across the expanse of the nighttime sky. Pure beauty—there were no other words for it.

She felt the shadow of her family's house retreat from her concerns, its buried lights and rambling form imperfect as memories, the gabled tower like a lighthouse on some craggy coast, surrounded by so much heavy wreckage. There were so many skeletons buried in these old woods. Now she could live the life she was meant to live, with him, together forever.

Orn had parked his battered Jeep on one of the rutted back roads. The sound of the hulking engine ripped through the night. They tore down the hill like they were in freefall, the dusty yellow headlights leading the way as the Jeep bounced and shook, catching the occasional eerie glow of some wild animal's eyes in the woods, lowdown and frozen in fear.

The thing that haunts people, Lettie thought, slipping through the vast unknown, is when they have a vision of completion, when they think they know what completion looks like, or have some idea of what it might feel like. Yet that vision remains unfinished. It's missing something. The haunting was the missing. It was the absence of God knew what.

She reached over and closed her hand around Orn's on the gear stick, threading their fingers together. She had everything she needed right here, everything she'd ever wanted in this boy. Orn's fingers were so much longer than hers. She squeezed tight—a perfect fit, skin on skin—and caught a glimpse of his widening smile in the dash light.

"It's you and me against the world." His words wrapped her up tight and held her secure, recalling oddly the flicking of Syd's forked tongue. Orn always said exactly what she wanted to hear in the simplest way. "We're stronger together."

She felt she was ready to die now. They shared the same

darkness, inside and out. She wanted to tattoo his name inside her heart.

They lapsed into a calm, comforting silence. Orn slid a tape into the deck and cranked the volume knob.

"I made this last night," he said over the first hints of fingerpicked acoustic guitar, a simple arpeggio in a minor chord. "Took two hits, stayed up, and watched the sunrise melt all over everything. Like watching the world get born again."

She closed her eyes. Clean electric guitar lines twined through the fingerpicking, first as complement, and then playing against the plucked rhythm, filling in the spaces between the notes.

"You took some of the new stuff tonight too, didn't you? I can see it in your eyes. You're about to spin off the Earth."

Lettie couldn't stop smiling. She loved the way drugs felt. What they showed her, the spaces that opened all around her. Outer space was an ocean in flux—a living pattern—and she bobbed along the surface of its cool waves. She loved the sound of rushing wind whipping through her head, the feeling of acceleration, blasting toward oblivion, each heartbeat radiating out into the beyond.

"Your brother sure knows his chemicals," Orn said. "He might even be a god someday."

They lapsed into another silence, not talking because there was nothing to say. All that mattered was being together, the music flowing over them, connecting them.

"Lettie, do you think I'm a freak?"

"A freak?"

"Do you think I'm dumb?"

He'd just failed the twelfth grade, and she knew that this bothered him far more than it bothered her. His family had a small but nice house in a quiet suburb, not some embarrassing old ruin out in the sticks. His dad had gone to college on a football scholarship, and even though he hadn't finished school or gone pro that still made him something in the eyes of others. His younger brother Scud was a football star in his own right, making varsity his freshman year. His mom was friends with everybody in town, even if she had a reputation for being an odd duck. His grandfather had even been the chief of police. They all seemed great to her—a real family without any missing pieces, without secrets. She hoped to know and love them all someday. She hoped they would welcome her and accept her for who she was.

"I think you're the smartest person I've ever met."

"I feel like a soft person. I feel too much."

"You're not—" She chose her words carefully. "I think there are all kinds of intelligence. What matters is being open to your feelings. It's not being soft. That's what makes you special. The way you feel things. You're sensitive. You're a very special person, Ornithan Bowles."

The intensity of the song increased, the two leads hinting at cataclysm, great washes of reverb and delay. The sound engulfed her, the atonality at times causing anxiety. Only then the pieces clicked into place, rippling tessellations of beauty.

"And you're a really good guitar player." She thought that saying anything more was unnecessary.

Orn swung the Jeep onto a narrow road that cut through the trees. They entered a clearing in the woods and rolled to a stop. He killed the engine.

"We're here."

They got to work. Lettie held the big yellow flashlight, watching

Orn set up the tent, adjusting the angle of light every so often. It seemed an immensely important job. A few minutes later, the tent was up and a small fire crackled within a ring of stones.

Orn stoked the flames with a long stick, sending up bursts of orange embers, streaks of light like so many fireflies. Lettie couldn't stop laughing. He handed her a warm can of beer—the satisfying click of the pull-tab, the hiss of the carbonation, foam running over her fingers. It tasted weirdly metallic, almost like the first time, back when she was eight or nine years old and she'd snuck a sip from a can of Bud.

The memory flared out into darkness, drifting away, ashen. Orn sat next to her and put one of his long arms around her small shoulders. She felt frail next to him. They sipped their beers and shared a few cigarettes, lighting new ones off the old ones, throwing the old ones into the fire. Then the flames started to die down, the heat-whitened logs smoldering, molten hearts.

The dark crept in around their campsite and their talk turned serious. Orn talked about their families, about how stupid their parents were. He talked about starting their new life together somewhere out west. No one could tell them what to do out there. No one could keep them apart. Orn crushed an empty beer can, pulled out a hip flask and took a long pull. He held it out to Lettie, but she shook her head. If he stayed around here, he said, he was going to shoot up the school. He talked about how much he hated his teachers and their classmates, about how his mother was suffocating him, how she was sucking the life out of him. The images in Lettie's head were horrible. She saw bodies full of bullet holes, crying children, blood gushing from open eyes, some black-winged demon descending from the writhing sky, arms out wide, inviting embrace. She started to freak out. Like, a lot. Orn got like this sometimes. Liquor made him moody, made him angry. He got carried away and forgot himself. He scared her when he fell into darkness. She couldn't handle other people's anger. She took too much of it in. She didn't want to be out here anymore. She wanted to be back in the warm light of her bedroom.

She missed her mom and dad. She was scared. It hurt so much. She felt so alone. Everything was happening so fast. She was too young to be out on her own. She was still a child who didn't like the taste of beer. She wished she could start her life over so she could get everything right. Everything had gone wrong—the cumulative effect of a lifetime of bad choices.

Where had she first gone wrong? What had she done? How did she get here? How did she get to this exact moment in time? To this particular place? The path behind her seemed so precarious. Would she ever find her way back?

Lettie had the overwhelming urge to pee. Her mind seemed sharp as ever, still functioning, but her body wouldn't respond. It was like she was trapped inside herself. How many beers had she had? She stumbled into the inky darkness, long black fingers threading together, pulling her in, suffocating her. The air away from the fire was shockingly cold. The nighttime woods were damp and rotting. She could hear the collective chatter of insects crawling through tiny wet tunnels.

Orn called her name as if she'd been lost for a long time, his voice frantic, echoing through the trees. He sounded like a ghost.

She found her way back to the blackened ring of stones, the fire now nearly dead. At some point their tent had collapsed. Orn was draped in pale moonlight. His mouth was all teeth. He was down in the dirt, sitting cross-legged, arm outstretched, an old switchblade pressed against his forearm. She saw the tip of the blade bite into his flesh, the bloom of crimson ribbon. He said he was going to prove to Lettie how much he loved her, slurring his speech. He was going to carve her name into his arm and then she would see how much he loved her. The blade kissed a straight line in his flesh that opened like a mouth, and she saw the flex of snakeskin in the newly lipped fold. She saw the skin beneath the skin. There was blood everywhere, black as pitch.

She tried to stop him, tried to wrestle away the knife. She screamed and cried. But he just kept saying over and over again that he needed to prove his love to her, that she shouldn't be scared of him. How could she be scared of him? Didn't she love him?

She was breaking his heart. She was killing him. Didn't she see that?

Nearly hysterical, Lettie balled her fists and beat on Orn's chest and face. She said that he was the dumbest person in the world. He couldn't even finish high school because he was so stupid. He ruined everything. He was a fuck-up. A loser. A failure. A freak.

A great wash of noise rustled through those old woods—the sound of hundreds of blackbirds suddenly taking flight. She was down on her knees in the cold mud, her face in her hands.

She heard the slam of a car door, the sound of Orn's Jeep roaring to life, a primal, furious sound. By the time she saw the headlights come on, the Jeep's oversized tires were already tearing down the narrow path back to the main road.

At first, she couldn't believe that he'd left her out there. It seemed impossible. She curled up in a ball near the lifeless remains of the fire and told herself that he wasn't really gone, that he'd be back soon, that this whole thing—whatever it was, whatever had just happened—was only a misunderstanding.

She spent an eternity like that. It wasn't until she felt herself coming down, her stomach bloated with rot. It wasn't until the sounds of the woods changed and the night bled away into the colorless early morning hours that she allowed herself to believe he wasn't coming back. She looked up to the quickly fading form of the Moon, the pale face of Selene, squinting, hiding herself away. And in that moment, she felt more alone than ever before.

A HOTEL ROOM BY THE HIGHWAY, THIRTEEN YEARS LATER

"Sorry, does the light bother your eyes?" The dark-haired woman adjusted the nearest box stand, trying to find the best angle for Lettie's features.

"It's fine." The tone of Lettie's voice said otherwise. This woman, the show's producer, had been trying to get the lighting right for nearly fifteen minutes, and Lettie finally had enough. "I just need to get some air."

Even with the sliding-glass window open—the winter air carrying the anxious hiss of the nearby highway—it was grossly hot in the overcrowded room. There were too many bodies too close together, everyone breathing, everyone sweating. The heat from the lights was inescapable. And the makeup on Lettie's face was so heavy it felt like a mask.

The producer shrugged, attempting to convey sympathy. It was such a minor gesture, but it was still meaningful. Lettie had always appreciated the little things, those unspoken connections between people. After all, this woman was everything Lettie was not: tall, stylish, confident.

Lettie got out of the armchair and went to the window, careful to step over the knotted electrical cords taped to the gray carpet. She sat on the long metal radiator and looked out below. Passing cars carved dark lines along the slushy, snow-littered highway, their tired yellow and red lights winking in the mist. In the far distance, the outlines of black-glass office complexes were barely visible, lumbering monoliths of mundanity. This was her world now, anonymous and colorless and cold.

Still, it was better than where she'd been. She had to remember that. She must remember that this was how she would earn her freedom once and for all.

"If you don't mind my asking," Lettie said, "how'd you get your nails to look like that?"

The producer pointed at herself, feigning surprise. Eyes wide, she mouthed the word, "Me?"

Yes, you. Who else? People who played stupid games truly had no understanding of the value of time.

"It's magnetic nail polish." The producer held out her hand so her fingers pointed to the floor like she was showing off an engagement ring. "They use magnets to pull the particles into a straight line, which gives it that cool streaking effect."

"Yeah, it's neat." Lettie inspected her own nails, plain and unpainted, cuticles chewed raw. "Nail polish was forbidden," she said, only half realizing she was talking out loud. "In prison, I mean." Suddenly self-conscious, she folded one hand over the other. There were so many things she had to relearn, how to talk to people, the rhythm of it, when to listen and when to speak, how to not say things that made her—and everyone else—want to curl up and die.

One of the crew guys, bulky and bearded in a black T-shirt, came over and handed Lettie a Styrofoam cup filled with coffee. "Thought you could use this. It's gonna be a long day."

She returned his smile and saw how he blushed, couldn't help but notice how quickly his eyes darted away from hers. He was scared of her. It seemed so absurd, considering his size, how much bigger than her he was. She saw that same look whenever people wondered if she was really dangerous, when they turned over in their minds what was fact and what was fiction.

The hotel room was a double. All the gear for the shoot was packed into black crates stacked on carts near the wardrobe. Grocery-store catering spreads had been placed on the desk in the far corner. Two armchairs had been arranged facing each other in the center of the room, and two large cameras on tripods had been carefully angled to capture the interview.

Lettie sipped the flavorless coffee. It scalded her tongue. She had just a moment to consider if she'd made a mistake when the bathroom door opened and out walked Barbara Shields, her blond hair done up like a pubescent pageant queen.

The famous primetime news anchor wore a paper makeup bib tucked into the collar of her shiny purple silk blouse. The makeup artist, the girl with the septum piercing and the red highlights in her jet-black hair, wasn't one for subtlety. Still, Lettie had to admit that Barbara looked just like she did on TV, just as she had for who knew how long, longer than Lettie had been alive, probably. The woman was freakishly ageless, radiating a dewy glow.

Barbara sat down in the armchair facing Lettie, crossed her nylon-smooth legs. She seemed so small, no bigger than a child. Her head was huge, though, maybe because of the hair.

When she spoke her voice was familiar, comforting. It was the soundtrack to millions of living rooms throughout the country. You can trust me, it said. You can open up to me.

"Thank you so much for your patience, Ms. Underhill. We'll get started in just a moment." Barbara turned and snapped her fingers at one of the crew guys, then turned her attention back to Lettie. "In the meantime, it might help if you told me what you hope to gain from this interview. After all, you've been a free woman for several weeks now. Why the sudden urge to speak out? Why today?"

Lettie drained the rest of the coffee and dropped the Styrofoam cup out the window, watched as it was swept away, twirling in the wind, forever lost in the endless white snow. She returned to her chair as she spoke. "In all honesty, I've been working on my book. Well, I've been talking to someone who's helping me write my book. You mentioned you read the chapter that was published in *Vanity Fair*? The response has been both—how can I say this? It's been both good and bad. What did that senator from Kansas say, exactly? That modern witchcraft was the biggest threat to our American way of life?"

"More so than the threat of terrorism," Barbara said, echoing the senator. Her voice went suddenly serious again. She really was an old pro. "Surely you know we attempted to contact you while you were incarcerated, yet you never returned our calls. Why?"

"There was a policy at the prison. You use your call to speak to a reporter and you forfeit your call from family and friends. And those calls were more important to me than anything."

"I was under the impression you received no phone calls while you were in prison, from family or otherwise. You're saying that isn't true?"

Lettie dropped her eyes to the floor and held her breath. It occurred to her that maybe these people knew more than they'd let on. They'd done their research. She needed to be more careful.

"There was always the chance, I guess, that someone might call. I never closed myself off to that possibility." She looked up again, met Barbara's gaze, and held it steady. "That sounds crazy to you, I know. But a person finds things to believe in when they're inside, things that keep them optimistic. It's how you survive."

"That's good. Let's use that in the interview."

Lettie got her breathing back under control. She'd have to do better when the real interview started. There was too much at stake.

"Ms. Underhill?" The bearded crew guy wavered in her periphery. "Sorry to interrupt. I need to attach your mic. We're ready to start."

She allowed him to do what he needed to do, the tip of his tongue visible in the corner of his mouth as he concentrated. He fumbled there for a moment too long before scuttling away, sheepish as ever. Lettie knew she had him under her spell. He was easy prey.

The red signal lamp above the camera opposite Lettie lit up. "Rolling," the operator said. The guy holding the boom repeated the same word.

Silence. The time had come. After all those long and lonely years, locked up and forgotten, Letitia Underhill could finally explain those horrible days that led to the infamous massacre. And unlike before, when the whole world followed her charade of a trial, that horrible parody of Salem's darkest days, everyone would have no choice but to listen to what she had to say.

"Thank you so much for agreeing to talk with us, Ms. Underhill,"

Barbara said. "Let's jump right in and start at the very beginning. How much do you remember about the day Ornithan Bowles disappeared?"

FRANKLYN BOWLES, THE DAY ORN DISAPPEARED

Ten minutes had passed since Frank first called upstairs that it was time for breakfast. If there was one thing in the world that got Orn out of bed, it was bacon frying in its own fat.

Court scraped at the pots and pans on the stove, muttering under her breath. Scud sat at the table, swallowing forkful after forkful of scrambled eggs, barely bothering to come up for air. Frank flipped disinterestedly through a week-old copy of the local paper, reading the crime blotter—everyone in their usual place, everything normal.

When Court finally ran out of patience, she sent Scud to go get his good-for-nothing brother. A minute later Scud came sauntering back into the kitchen with a wry smile on his face.

"He's not in his room. I checked everywhere."

Fuck, Frank thought. Here we go.

Orn's increasingly reckless behavior had been the subject of many heated discussions between Frank and Court. The way Frank saw it, Orn was just exorcising teenage demons. Hell, the boy's transgressions—sneaking booze, smoking weed, staying out late—weren't so different from the shit he'd pulled at that age. But Court knew well enough what kind of trouble teenage boys got themselves into, and she knew—or thought she knew—that something worse had taken hold of her oldest.

Court left the bacon sizzling in the pan and stormed out to the garage. She came back madder than hell. Orn's Jeep was gone. Then the interrogation began. First, she focused on Scud: When was the last time you heard from him? Where'd he say he was going? Who's he been hanging out with? And then she turned to Frank: Why so quiet? Nothing to say?

No, nothing he could say would calm her down any. He just kept on reading his paper, sighing every so often. Orn didn't have a cellphone yet, even though he was always begging for one. They were too expensive and coverage was patchy. Court tried a bunch of his friends—called their houses, even called some of their moms at their jobs. No luck.

The bacon was burning by then, filling the kitchen with acrid, greasy smoke. Court killed the burner, pulled the pan, and tossed it into the sink.

She pursued Frank and Scud into the living room, where Hunter was just waking up, wearing the same jeans and work shirt as yesterday. He'd been camped out on the couch for the past two months, ever since he'd been paroled.

Hunter sat up like he'd been caught sleeping on the job. Beer bottles covered the coffee table. He smelled like he'd had about six too many the night before, fumbled around, clanking glass, until he found his smokes. "What's going on?"

If ever there was an example of self-destructive teenage impulses resulting in a lifetime of horrific tragedy, it was Frank's brother-in-law, Hunter Holbrook.

"Are you touched?" Court reached out and plucked the cigarette from Hunter's mouth. "No smoking in the goddamn house." She ripped the cigarette in half and jammed the pieces down the neck of a half-full beer bottle.

From the corner of his eye, Frank saw Scud dash back to the kitchen and slip out the side door. At least the boy was smart enough to know when to disappear. Surely that was a skill that would serve him well in life.

"The state of this place," Court said.

Hunter's dirty clothes were piled up on the recliner, the fireplace mantle, the windowsills. Grease-stained pizza boxes and 7-11 containers were stacked on the floor. The room was skunked with stale smoke, stale sweat, and stale beer.

"No wonder Orn's drinking and staying out all night, the example you set."

Hunter put his hands up in the air. "The fuck did I do?"

Frank stepped between them. "The boy didn't come home last night. Get up and let's see if we can't find where he's at." He turned to Court. "Listen, I'm sure he's fine. He's probably just crashed at a friend's place, sleeping it off. You know how it is."

He hoped to God he sounded like he believed what he said, but damned if he didn't suddenly feel something dark come to pass.

Court fumed. "I do, don't I? Know how it is. That's the goddamn truth." She looked older than ever. Frank's heart ached for her as she retreated to the kitchen, shuffling her steps, shoulders rounded.

Frank and Hunter left through the front door, crossed the yard, and slid into Frank's old black Cadillac.

"She is a pain in my ass," Hunter said as the car's cavernous V8 came alive.

The opening chords of AC/DC's "Hells Bells" played on the radio. Hunter threw on his stupid wraparound sunglasses, same style Oakleys he wore before he got sent up. He looked like an asshole, but Frank didn't have the heart to tell him.

"You been driving my car again?" Frank adjusted the position of the driver's seat, sliding away from the steering wheel, straightening the seatback.

Hunter said nothing, just kept looking out the window.

"Look, you take it out, you fill it up. Put the seat back where it was. Why is that so hard?"

The car surged as it pulled away from the curb.

"That's another thing. Don't talk shit about your sister to me. She's dealing with a lot lately, not the least of which is your ass not being able to find work."

Hunter dropped his seat so far back he was nearly lying down. He lit a cigarette and cracked the window. "You try getting a job with a record like mine, see how easy it is. My PO is riding my ass. You two are always on my case. I'm getting shot from both sides."

Maybe Court was right about Hunter being a bad example, about where Orn was picking up his bad behavior. He had to be learning it from somewhere. The thought that Orn might wind up like Hunter someday made Frank want to punch in the dash radio.

"Look, it's my fucking house. Clean up your shit."

There wasn't much else to say. Hunter turned away once again, resigned to watch the world go by.

They cruised to the end of the block, hung a right, and continued along the quiet, tree-lined suburban streets. Early summer was in full bloom. The flavorful smoke from Hunter's cigarette mingled with the smells of ragweed and freshly cut grass. This time of year always reminded Frank of those endless offseason practice sessions. The sound of young men in full padding colliding out on the field, hitting the sled, running laps. God, it brought back memories— the best years of his life.

As they got closer to town, the yards got smaller before they disappeared altogether, replaced by so much concrete. The sidewalks fell into disrepair. They passed chain-link fences with their gates hanging loose, an ugly stretch of boarded-up houses, an abandoned strip mall. Everything was old, falling apart.

Stone River had seen better days, that much was certain, but Frank still loved this place. It killed him to think that only twenty years ago there were car dealerships all over town, lots packed tight with brand new cherry-red paint jobs. Now, the streetlights didn't turn on after dark. Animal control trucks prowled back alleys, steel cages packed with wild, abandoned mutts, gnashing yellowed teeth. Kids got caught with drugs at school. A bunch of the oldest churches were boarded up.

Frank's family had been there since the beginning, through good times and bad, even had the name tree and birth certificates to prove it. Hell, his dad had basically run the whole town before he started building fancy lake houses for out of towners.

Back in the day, the commercial coal-mining boom put Stone River on the map. Turns out the whole place sat atop massive beds of Pennsylvanian rock. Thousands of lost souls traveled up the Mississippi from St. Louis, some from as far away as Memphis, others from New Orleans. That meant there were a lot of folks who saw things differently. They didn't get along so well. There was lawlessness back then, and the worst crimes left wounds that never quite healed. But the coal brought in good money, even made a few families rich.

Then the mines dried up, just like they always do. Most people went chasing after work. The harsh Illinois winters drove away nearly everyone else. Now, Stone River was little more than a name in the registry of historical places. Main Street still had a pulse, just barely, but there wasn't much else to speak of. There were two diners that served decent coffee, a Wal-Mart out by the highway, a Civil War monument even though there were no battles fought in the whole state.

The real point of pride was the three-time state champ varsity football team, with Scud its next starting tight end. Signs of support were everywhere. You couldn't escape them. Frank pulled into a parking spot right in front of one: a blue-and-gold banner, an anthropomorphized bobcat flexing its bicep, its upper lip curled.

Scud took after his old man. He was built like a truck, square-jawed, a natural-born bruiser. Orn took after his mother. He couldn't put on weight if he tried. Other kids fucked with him. He got teased a lot growing up and it messed with his head.

"This is a waste of time," Hunter said. "You ever talk to your son? He hates this fucking place."

Frank shot him a look—the one. That was that.

It was the middle of first period and the halls were empty. They made their way to the front office, where Frank asked the receptionist if there was someone he could speak with. As soon as he mentioned the name Ornithan Bowles, the whole room went quiet. A minute later, the guidance counselor came out, introduced himself, shook their hands.

Turns out Orn hadn't been to school in weeks. He was failing all of his classes, even art, which was his strongest subject. They caught him smoking in the bathroom, found a knife in his gym locker. He didn't respond when his teachers called on him in class. He was standoffish. He threatened to break some kid's nose. The school called home and left messages. They mailed a letter and received signatures from both parents in return.

Frank's head spun. He felt like he couldn't breathe, more embarrassed than he was angry, though he was plenty angry. Orn hadn't been going to school, but he still left the house every morning. So, where was he going? How was he spending his time? And who was he spending it with?

He honestly didn't remember what he said—or how the rest of the conversation went—he had to get out of that place as quickly as he could. He had to get some air. Fuck, he felt like he was choking. What in God's name would he tell Court?

Back in the Cadillac, pulling out of the parking lot, the building in the rearview mirror getting smaller. Frank lost himself in the confusion of stoplights and the occasional flare of sunlight off passing cars.

"I told you, man," Hunter said. "Orn fucking hates that place."

"What do you know about it?"

"Look, I know you're angry. And I know that's not gonna help anything. We gotta think this through. Be smart."

Frank focused on his breathing, tried to clear his thoughts, both things he'd learned in the anger-management classes he'd taken at the beginning of his marriage, back when he and Court had nearly split, when he was downing a pint of Canadian Club on his way home from work. He pictured dark waves crashing against a black-sand beach, calm, rhythmic. He thought about what life would be like on the Moon. A black sea. What did they call it—

the Sea of Tranquility? How appropriate.

He remembered when Court first told him she was pregnant with Orn. It had instantly given his life meaning. Fuck football. Orn's impending birth made everything make sense. Every day since then had been an increasingly desperate attempt at sustaining that feeling, and now it was unraveling. His worst fear.

"School is for dipshits," Hunter said. "Orn is too cool for that shit. You know what I mean?" He paused, lit another cigarette. "Remember where the cool kids hung out when we were in school? Some things never change, man. You know what I mean?"

There was an abandoned limestone quarry just outside of town, two square miles of sheer cliffs, winding roads, and deep pools of clear water. Kids hung out there, fucked around, and got high. All summer long there were endless bonfires beneath the stars. On a clear night, you could see all the way to Mars.

There was a service road that followed the rusted fence at the quarry's edge. Frank's Cadillac left huge clouds of chalky dust in its wake, crunching gravel, the afternoon sun burning high and white. They ignored the bullet-hole-ridden "no trespassing" sign and drove up the main road, took the ramp near one of the central rock mounds. From there they had a clear view of everything, miles in every direction. This was a place outside of time, unchanging, flattened forever by titanic glaciers.

Somebody had lugged a mattress up there. It was waterlogged, covered in spray paint and strips of duct tape. All around the mattress were crushed beer cans, shards of broken glass glittering in the sun, a bright yellow condom.

"What'd I tell you?" Hunter said, poking at the condom with a stick. "Nothing ever changes. You ever fuck my sister up here?"

Frank ignored him, scanned the grounds below, making a visor with his fingers to block out the sun. "Over there." He pointed with his other hand.

They left the car behind and carefully made their way down the slope of the rock mound. The kids saw them coming from maybe a hundred yards out, but they didn't make a move, total burnouts, probably bombed out of their minds on whatever it was kids smoked or snorted these days.

There were four of them: three boys and a girl, all in their mid to late teens. All of them wore black: skater shoes and Doc Martens, baggy pants, Marilyn Manson T-shirts. One of them even wore a black trench coat and a stupid hat, a trilby. Two smoked hand-rolled cigarettes. Another held a half-full bottle of red wine by its neck. The fourth one leaned back against a fire-gutted steel drum, arms crossed over his chest. He looked like he hadn't eaten in days.

"Any of you know Ornithan Bowles?" Frank asked.

The kids exchanged inscrutable looks. One of them spat something that looked like blood.

"We're not cops," Hunter said.

"No shit," said the one with the wine bottle.

"I know who you are," another one said, nodding to Hunter.

"Yeah? It's a small town."

The kid smiled. His teeth were jacked.

"Listen, I'm Orn's dad. We don't know where he's at and we need to find him. If any of you have seen him—if you know anything—it would really help us out."

Again, the kids looked at one another. Frank felt his pulse quicken. He was ready to pick up the one in the hat and start swinging him around. These were the kinds of kids he used to terrorize back in high school. Now he remembered why.

"Orn used to hang out here sometimes." The girl tilted her head slightly. "He came around with some other kids, but he hasn't been around lately."

"Know why? Where he's been?"

"He got himself a girlfriend, started spending all his time with her."

Another one added, "He's with Letitia Underhill."

At first, Frank thought he'd misheard. That couldn't possibly be true. There was no way Orn was seeing an Underhill. It was impossible. He looked at Hunter, emotionless as ever, eyes hidden behind those goddamned wraparound sunglasses. Christ. Those families who got rich from coal back in the day and helped build the town? The Underhills had been the richest of them all. And Frank's family had a long, sordid history with them. Surely these kids knew that. Surely they were just fucking with him.

"Orn was dating this Underhill girl? You guys sure about that?"

"Of course," the girl said, as if it were the most obvious thing in the world. Then she explained that everyone called Orn's girlfriend Lettie. She was a year younger than him, a junior, and they were totally inseparable. "It's actually pretty gross. They got together last summer at one of the bonfires, then they stopped coming around. After that, it was almost like Orn fell off the face of the Earth. They cut themselves off from everything and everyone, lived in their own little world. She's totally obsessed."

Frank and Hunter killed the rest of the day driving aimlessly around town. Neither of them said a word. They listened to the radio. This was bad, really bad. Hunter burned through his cigarettes. The hours went by in a blur.

By the time they pulled up in front of the house, Frank half expected Orn's Jeep to be parked in the garage, for Orn to be home, up in his room, hunched in front of the computer playing *Quake* or *Unreal* or whatever he was into that month. He'd be mad because his mom yelled at him, but he'd be home. Everything back to normal. Except it wasn't. Orn wasn't home. There'd been no sign of him all day, no call, nothing.

Hunter cracked the first of what would be many beers that night and returned to his spot on the couch. Scud kept to his room, the door shut tight. Nothing had changed, but it felt like everything had changed.

Court was inconsolable. Frank held her in their bed and let her cry. He told her everything he'd learned. Orn had taken up with an Underhill girl and flunked out of school. It was impossible, all of it, every last little detail. Court kept saying over and over again that she knew something was horribly wrong. This proved it. She lowered her voice. This was how those evil fucking Underhills would get their revenge for the accident. This was how they would pay them back for Sweet Lou. And when Frank once again suggested that Orn was probably just out with his friends, blowing off steam, pissed off about something or other, Court put her hand over his mouth and silenced him with her eyes.

"A mother knows. A mother always knows."

He let her have that. Who was he to argue with that?

They held each other as the seconds ticked away. The sound of Court's breathing deepened, slowed down, and soon enough she fell asleep.

Frank held his wife, listening to the sound of her breathing, the rhythm of it, his thoughts returning to that black-sand beach somewhere far away—the Sea of Tranquility—its waves receding, rushing forward, receding once more. Surely it existed somewhere out there in all that unending space.

The fucking Underhills. He couldn't believe it. It always came back to them.

He felt a weight pushing out against the front of his skull from behind his eyes. He couldn't remember the last time he'd cried, and he sure as shit wasn't going to start now.

MARGARET UNDERHILL, EARLIER THAT DAY

Peg grabbed one of the hunting rifles, the Ultra Lux, and went out back. She was determined to kill the rabbits that had got into the lettuce patch, the ones that had chewed right through the fence, the little pests. Lettuce was such a delicate plant, difficult to sow in the soil. It needed to be looked after.

She threw the bolt on the rifle, the sound of machined precision, gliding the copper jacket. The blood-orange sun arched over the tree line at the edge of the property. Peg didn't care what anybody else said: dusk was the best time for hunting rabbits. Dawn was wired with fear, every living creature on high alert, the beginning of yet another dance with death. Dusk was when the world let its guard down. Everything went lazy. That's when the killing was good.

Peg went out back and let the family's two shepherds—Kate and Minnie—out of their kennel. The dogs bolted past her, nearly knocking her over, raced to the fields, barking at whatever it was they were chasing, field mice or butterflies.

She left through the gate and followed the path to the creek bed. There, she split off between two hills, oak trees on one side, elm on the other. She heard the dogs barking in the distance, far away now. A light wind gently rustled the leaves overhead, the sound so similar to falling water, soothing and peaceful. She took a moment to close her eyes and appreciate it, to let the wind flow over her. Then she climbed the slope of staggered, mulchy railroad ties, passed one of the shadowy mine entrances—long ago boarded up and abandoned, exhaling the subtle reek of cool, earthen air— and entered an endless, dandelion-choked field.

From there she had a clear view of House Underhill's sprawling ruin, whole sections crushed beneath vegetation, wrestled down by creeping vines and crawling ivy. At one point it had been the largest house in all of Stone River, home to generations. Now, only Peg and the twins lived within its damp, discolored walls, occupying only a few of its many rooms, cornered by the steady onslaught of earwigs and slugs, the slow spread of black mold and water damage.

It was an odd, ugly structure. The big house had been built on top of another house, a smaller house, an older house, which itself was built on top of the original mining outpost. And none of those buildings quite fit. Inside there were strange seams where the walls and floors and ceilings didn't quite come together. There were hallways that went nowhere, rooms inside of rooms, floors built between floors. It felt like several people had taken on the task of putting the house together, each of whom lost interest halfway through.

Still, the house told Peg who she was, and in this she found a sense of pride. She was an Underhill. And when the thought of this threatened to overwhelm her emotions, overtake her senses, she left the field and followed the creek back to the main grounds, where she crept quietly through the grass.

Just before dark, one of the skinny rabbits scurried under the fence, hopping into range. Peg's eyesight wasn't what it used to be, but it didn't matter. She had a feel for guns and an intuition for killing. It was in her nature. She let the shape of the animal fill the sight of the scope and firmly squeezed the trigger. The tight shot of the Ultra Lux phased through the hills like a low summer storm, barely kicking back. Best rabbit-hunting rifle in the world. She spent three more cartridges before she was done. On her way in, Peg whistled to the dogs. A moment later they joined her.

Night fell. The kitchen windows shone like black gems in the low, warm light. Peg arranged the cooked rabbit on an engraved silver platter, mixed up a bowl of fresh greens and diced tomatoes from the garden, and filled a glass pitcher with unsweetened iced tea.

Stephen got there first, emerging from the basement, his jeans and T-shirt streaked with mud, hair caked with dust. He wore the furtive look of a rodent. Peg glared at him, told him to wash his hands and take his dirty shoes out to the porch to dry. She set down the food for the dogs, watched them eat greedily, pushing the dishes along the floor.

Lettie came down from her room not long after, eyes swollen like she'd been crying. The girl had taken to slamming doors and talking back, not acting her normal self at all.

Peg took a deep breath. She loved the twins as her own, she did, but she also found them exhausting. They were both impulsive and headstrong. They reminded her too much of her own damn self.

Stephen hunched forward, held his fork in his closed fist like some kind of caveman. Lettie sat with her knees bent, wearing brightly colored soccer shorts, her thin legs folded against her chest. She tried to hide herself inside her oversized hooded sweatshirt, but there was no escaping Peg's attention—not at the supper table.

"You didn't go to school today. What's the matter with you?"

"Nothing's the matter with me." Lettie exaggerated each word. She picked up a rabbit thigh and started peeling it apart, tearing free small hunks of lean meat, squeezing out droplets of clear juice between two fingers, skin white with pressure. She rolled the dried-out bits of meat into tight little balls.

Peg watched as Lettie fed the little balls to Kate and Minnie, both of them whining, pawing at the girl, watched her go about further tearing the meat into little strands, then ripping those strands into smaller and smaller pieces. Sometimes it was like she lived with two terrifying strangers.

"What in God's name is this? Squirrel?"

"Rabbit." Peg didn't much appreciate the girl's tone. "Skinned them myself."

"I heard the gunshots," Stephen said, his mouth full. "Figured you were out there killing something."

"What a genius." Lettie made a scene of smelling her fingers, glistening with sticky, clear fluids. She twisted up her face. "Why can't we just order pizza like normal people? Other people eat fried chicken. They eat hamburgers. Sloppy Joes. They don't kill wild animals in their front yards and make their grandkids eat them. These things carry diseases?"

"You've eaten rabbit hundreds of times and never once complained."

Lettie wiped her hand on her napkin. She pushed her plate

forward, dropped her feet to the floor, and slid down in her chair. Peg wanted to smack some sense into her, but knew better. Kids these days were likely to call the cops.

The dogs lost interest. Kate went off to her bed in the living room, while Minnie shoved her way past Peg's chair, lying on her side beneath the table, near everyone's feet.

Peg turned her attention to Stephen. "What were you doing in the basement that got you so dirty?"

"Crawlspace."

Peg raised an eyebrow, waited for him to continue. When it was clear he wasn't going to, she asked him to be more specific.

"Just exploring. There's a whole world down there, you know."

Peg paused for a moment, remembering the stories her father used to tell her about the passageways beneath the house, how some of them connected to the old coal mines, how others led to the deep crags of Copper Creek. She'd heard stories of cave-ins and worse: men buried alive, wild stories of survival, hauntings in the dark, the souls of coal miners trapped in suffocating tombs. On quiet nights, she sometimes heard strange sounds from down below, not unlike voices, moans of agony, the chattering of teeth and fractured minds. Those sounds, those voices, filled her with a dread that was beyond description. She couldn't say why. She just knew they were the sounds of things better left alone.

"There something down there in particular you're looking for?"

Stephen shrugged, kept working at his food. "Just exploring, that's all."

"I buy you those chemistry books you're always asking for. I get you a library's worth of books every couple months. And still, you insist on crawling around in the dark like some kind of human mole."

She made sure he looked her in the eyes. "Stay out of the basement. It's not safe. A lot of those old passageways were bricked over for a reason."

Stephen glared at her, nodded silently.

Lettie sighed.

"That sighing got something to do with where you took off to last night?"

The girl's eyes went wide. She had a bad habit of thinking she was smarter than everyone, as if her grandmother wouldn't hear her stomping around on the roof in the middle of the night. The house's high ceilings, old staircases, and long hallways carried noise all too well. A single floorboard creaking in the still of the night could be loud as a scream. She'd done a bad job these past few years of letting the twins run wild, up at all hours, getting into trouble.

"You two—listen up. Your days of wine and roses are over. You're both old enough now. It's time you get summer jobs, start chipping in."

Both Lettie and Stephen ignored her.

Peg balled her fist and pounded the table to get their attention. They both jumped in their seats. "From now on we share what's going on in our lives. From now on we talk to each other."

Lettie was frozen with fear. Tears welled in her eyes.

"I'm not mad about you sneaking out, if that's what you're thinking. I'm worried that maybe you're in trouble. Are you pregnant?"

"Oh my God." Lettie laughed nervously. "Is that really what you think?"

Peg didn't know what to think. She threw her hands up in the air in frustration. These two would be the death of her.

"Tell her," Stephen said, carefully laying down his knife and fork. In that moment he sounded more adult than ever, an eerie echo of his dad.

"Shut up, Stephen."

The twins held each other's gaze—one of those strange moments of theirs. They had an odd connection, those two, something powerful and scary. It was particularly unnerving when the twins were little, before they'd gotten good at being discreet.

The air crackled with currents of electricity, carrying hints of charcoal and smoke.

"Is something burning?" Peg looked back to the kitchen. The stovetop was off, oven too.

"You can't hide it anymore," Stephen said. "Tell her."

"Jesus Christ." A tear slowly streamed down Lettie's cheek, then another. "There's nothing to tell, Stephen."

Peg looked to each of them. Their eyes always told the truth. Suddenly she sensed that something had been set in motion, something bad. She quickly did the math: How many years had it been?

Stephen turned to his grandmother. "She's in love with Ornithan Bowles."

"Shut the fuck up, Stephen." Lettie pushed away from the table, breaking the connection with her brother, her teeth clenched, face red with rage.

Minnie woke up from her slumber under the table, started barking.

"Hey—" Peg said, but Lettie ignored her, storming out of the kitchen. The dog chased after her, paws treading against the wood floor.

A moment later, from deep within the house, Peg heard Lettie's bedroom door slam shut. The Bowles boy? Could it really be true?

She heard the distant sounds of two cars colliding—the crunch of bone—screams that echoed in the night.

"You gonna tell me what that was all about?" Peg felt sick to her stomach. She'd already lost so much. She couldn't bear to lose anything else.

"It's not my place," Stephen said. He picked up his silverware, solemnly stabbed the last piece of rabbit with his fork. "You're gonna have to ask her yourself."

Later that night, Peg knocked on Lettie's door. And when she didn't get a response, she pushed it open, hinges creaking. A blade of light widened across the floor, revealing Lettie lying face down on her bed. Quiet music played on her stereo, the gentle brushing of an acoustic guitar, a young man's breathy voice.

Minnie was sprawled out at the foot of the bed. "Move over," Peg said, sitting down next to the dog. Lettie didn't react and neither did the dog.

A full minute passed before Peg leaned over and pressed the power button on the stereo. Lettie rolled over, positioned herself with her back against the headboard. She hugged a small stuffed unicorn to her stomach.

"We're going to the woods," Peg said. "I don't care if you're tired. You and I are going for a walk. Make sure you put on long pants and wear long sleeves." And then, "There's something I need to show you."

The beam of Peg's flashlight swept over the thorny, tangled branches, the gently sloping ground slicked with mud, everything still drying out from the long winter. They kicked away dead leaves as they carefully slid between trees, climbed over rotting logs. Crickets hummed and bullfrogs barked, sometimes joined by the weird, vibratory call of a screech owl. It was slow going, and it was dark. Only the occasional strand of silver moonlight snuck through the tree cover.

Peg stopped at the foot of a particularly large cottonwood tree, its trunk hideously gnarled. The thing had to be more than a thousand years old, with an equal number of branches, each snaking toward the sky. She swept away some dead leaves, ripped up clumps of clinging moss, and revealed a wide tree stump, its blackened, misshapen form hardened by time. Then she reached into her jacket pocket and took out a rabbit pelt—clots of blood still clinging to its rough fur—and placed it on the stump's flat surface. She muttered a few words under her breath, just enough to pay service.

This day always had to come, she knew that. Children need to know where they're from. They need to know where they belong. And it's left to mothers to teach them, because the real power, the thing that survives through the ages, is always bestowed upon girls by women.

"What is this?" Lettie said, finding a seat on a fallen tree. "Why did you bring me out here?"

Peg clicked off the light and let the darkness settle. "Your mother loved it here, Letitia. She used to come out here on nights just like this one and recite the names of your ancestors, the ones who died violent deaths. Some were hanged. Others were hunted down and burned alive. Others drowned or were thrown off cliffs. The world simply wouldn't let them be who they were."

Peg could just barely make out the girl's outline in the dark, sniffling, wiping her nose with her sleeve. Once more, the sound of a screech owl trilling.

"I know you know the power you have. I know you feel it coursing through your veins. I felt it tonight. Maybe you're tempted to use it. I can't say I'd blame you. But I want you to know that you are not alone. There were others before you—many others. Some were forced to hold their tongues as the flames licked the soles of their feet."

"I don't know what—"

"For now, you listen. These are important things I need to tell you, things I didn't know how to tell you when you were little, you and your brother." Peg took a deep breath. "Your parents died in a car accident, that much is true, but it's only half the truth. The fact is they were killed by a man named Hunter Holbrook." She paused for a moment, let the name sink in. "You know who he is, don't you? I thought you might. He's the one who robbed your mom—my sweet little girl—of her life. He's the one who took her and your daddy away from us."

Lettie remained shrouded in darkness, only now she'd gone still, quiet. Peg felt something radiating from the girl, a strange force, ripples of anger and intensity.

"How?"

Peg waved away the question. "The police said it was an accident. They said he lost control of his car. They kept his name out of the news. And now he's a free man. Now he gets to walk the Earth while your parents lie dead and buried." Another deep breath. "All you need to know is that he's one of them—a Bowles. That's why they protected him. He's one of them who have done grievous harm to us Underhills—a single link in a chain that binds our families together. I know you know the stories. It's how it's always been, one tragedy after another, one accident after another. But now you need to know how it affects you. It's what drew you to that boy—I'm sure of it—this thing between our families."

"You mean about the feud?"

"It's something worse than that, I'm afraid."

Lettie seemed to think about this for a moment. "Like what?"

Peg stayed quiet.

"Does Stephen know about all this? About our parents?"

"No. You've always been quicker than your brother, Letitia. You always catch on to things faster than him. You're growing up faster. The women in our family always do. Your brother isn't ready yet. He's still a boy. He's liable to do something he'll regret."

"You really think so?"

"Yes. All Underhills eventually learn the secrets of their blood. Stephen will learn when he's ready. This is the burden we bear. For now, I need you to know I'm worried you'll suffer the burden so long as you keep this boy in your life. You might think you love him. You might even believe it. But you don't understand what that means. Someday you will. But for now you simply cannot see him anymore. Your very life depends on it."

Suddenly Lettie was on her feet, pressing her hot face into the line of her grandmother's neck. Peg wrapped her arms around the girl, held her as she cried.

She let it out in bursts, pulling in air when she could, repeating over and over again that she hated Orn, that he'd left her out in the woods alone in the dark, scared and cold and all alone in the world. She said that she never wanted to see him again. And then—just like that—it was like she found relief where before there had only been sadness and confusion. Lettie took a step back, once more wiping her eyes with her sleeve.

Peg would have given anything in that moment to peer through the night, to see the truth that her granddaughter's eyes held. But she couldn't. There was nothing there, just the dark. And when the girl spoke, her voice was cold and mean.

"I'll never forget who my family is. So long as I live, I'll never forget."

A HOTEL ROOM BY THE HIGHWAY

"I'm sorry," Lettie said, waving her hands in front of her eyes. "I don't want to ruin my makeup."

"Of course." Barbara remained perfectly composed. "Take all the time you need."

The signal lamp above the camera went out—the operator rubbed the back of his neck and exhaled loudly—and with it, Lettie felt an immense pressure lift. She could be herself again. She could breathe again. The intensity of telling this story had taken her by surprise, the sheer amount of recall involved, synthesizing everything she'd learned during the trial, from reading the news, sifting through her memories, re-experiencing those horrible feelings, all the research she'd done before starting her book.

So much time had passed, so many years. Why was it still so difficult to talk about her grandmother? It worried her that her emotions had flared out of control this early in the interview. Even worse, there was more to come, and much of it would be tougher to tell.

The box lights cut, the industrial snap of a flipped fuse switch, and the temperature in the room immediately plunged five degrees. Where before there had been concentration and quiet, the break brought with it motion and noise. Someone opened the window, the steady hiss of the highway swirling through the room. The dark-haired producer immediately went back to fussing with the lights. The crew started chatting among themselves, picking at the sliced meats, crackers, and cheese cubes. And the makeup girl flocked to Barbara Shields, who asked anyone within earshot for a bottle of water.

The bearded crew guy didn't miss a beat. He approached Lettie as soon as he could, just as she knew he would. "Here you go." He offered up a box of tissues. "Let me know if there's anything else you need. There's a vending machine down the hall. It's got candy bars and chips. Famous Amos. Funyuns—those are my favorite. I can get whatever you want."

"Thank you." Lettie carefully dabbed at her eyes with a tissue. "You're very sweet."

His face flushed red. He wet his lips, breathing rapidly, working up the nerve. "My name's Mark, by the way." He looked around to see if anyone was watching—if anyone appeared to be listening—and decided it was safe to keep talking to her. "I just wanted to let you know that you're doing a great job. I know it's gotta be tough."

"Thank you," Lettie said again. She gave him her most genuine smile and his whole face lit up. She could give his heart a tight squeeze and he'd drop dead on the spot. But before Lettie could say anything else, the makeup girl was there, inserting herself between them.

"Your turn," the girl said. She used a Q-tip to pat around Lettie's eyes.

"Did that hurt? The thing in your nose?"

The makeup girl said nothing. She ran a small powder brush along Lettie's cheekbones, the bridge of her nose, penciled below her eyes.

Barbara took a sip from the plastic bottle of water and set it on the floor. She clapped her hands a single time and the room snapped to attention. "Are we ready, folks?"

Lettie wondered what had happened to taking all the time she needed. Part of her didn't care. She wanted to get this over with as soon as possible. Yet another part of her couldn't help but feel slighted. This was her story. She was the one suffering to tell it. She was the one who had been made to sacrifice everything, all those years, her youth. She'd given up everything—and for what? To be cast out of society? To be locked away in a hole in the ground and forced to fend for herself among murderers and junkies?

Somebody closed the window, returning the room to grave stillness. The box lights ignited once more. Everyone returned to their positions, hovering just beyond the superheated glow, still as shadows, specters just beyond the reach of Lettie's vision. The red signal lamp followed.

She saw that Mark had taken his place in the back of the room by the gear. He watched with his arms folded across his chest.

"Rolling," the camera operator said, echoed once more by the guy holding the boom.

Lettie quickly focused on her breathing, tried to calm herself. She needed to stay calm. And if she couldn't manage that, she needed to at least appear calm.

Barbara tilted her head slightly. "Tell me, how is it you seem to know so much? For instance, you seem to have access to a great number of details about the personal lives of the Bowles family."

"Well, Orn told me a lot. I mean, he told me basically everything—up until he went missing. And I've been working on a book about all of this for quite some time now. I started writing it after my trial. It's been slow going, if you can imagine. So I've had a lot of time to put the pieces together." She paused. "God knows when I'll finish it."

Barbara switched gears. "Ornithan Bowles was your first love. It's often been said that the reason your story caught the attention of the public—the reason it gained a national audience, captured its collective imagination—was because it was reminiscent of the great dramas. Romeo and Juliet. Pyramus and Thisbe. Young love eclipsed by two families locked in a terrible feud, which then gave way to unspeakable tragedy. It's a story we tell ourselves again and again."

Lettie didn't know how to react. She smiled weakly, nodded as Barbara continued. She couldn't tell if this was going to lead to a question, or what the purpose—

"Can you tell us how you felt when you first learned that Orn went missing?"

And there it was. She was prepared for this one. "Of course. I felt the way any teenage girl would feel. I felt abandoned, like no one understood me. I felt like nobody had ever experienced the kind of connection Orn and I had. Honestly, part of me still believes that. Part of me still believes that our love was special." She paused, channeled a look of consternation, something she'd practiced in the mirror a thousand times. "Orn struggled with depression. I didn't realize it then, but I know now that he self-medicated with drugs and alcohol. He was trying to get better the only way he knew how. So when he went missing—this will sound terrible, but it's true—my first thought was that he had committed suicide."

Barbara didn't miss a beat. "Had he ever expressed suicidal thoughts to you before?"

"Yes. He told me that it would have been better if he'd never been born. He resented that he was never given a choice in the matter. He resented the very idea that he existed in the world, like he was somehow complicit in other people's pain, responsible somehow. He felt so much for other people. We both did."

Had Orn actually expressed resentment at being born? She couldn't remember. Not everything she said had to be the truth. It sounded like something Orn would have said, and that was all that mattered. This was her story. She could tell it however she wanted.

"Did you ever see Orn hurt himself? Did he practice self-harm?"

"Yes. The night of his disappearance, he cut himself. That much is documented, of course. He cut my name into his arm. There are photos. I'm saying here today that he did that to himself. Definitively. A lot of people think I wanted him to do that, or that I convinced him to, but I would never have asked him to hurt himself. In fact, I tried to stop him that night and he yelled at me. That's what we fought about." She paused. "He scared me when he got like that. It was like he was someone else."

"Was he ever violent toward you?"

"No. Absolutely not."

Barbara nodded. "Three days after he went missing, authorities discovered Orn's Jeep in the woods. Blood found on the driver's seat and steering wheel was a match—AB-positive. The keys were still in the ignition." She paused for a beat. "Two weeks passed. School let out. At your grandmother's insistence, you started a part-time job at the grocery store in town. Is that correct?"

"Yes, that's correct."

"This was your first job?"

"Still my only job."

"And that was when Orn's mother confronted you?"

Lettie nodded. That day in the grocery store had also been well documented during the trial. Witnesses were brought forth, testimonies given. All of it made Lettie look very, very bad.

If there was one thing she wished to undo in this whole series of unfortunate events, it would be what she said to Orn's mother that day. Only later did she come to realize this, and in the worst possible way. Maybe things would have turned out differently.

"I deeply regret my actions that day," Lettie said, meaning every word. "And I equally regret my testimony regarding those actions during the trial. I was scared. I thought that if I made myself look mean—if I could look strong and powerful—people might be less inclined to say the kinds of things they said about me. I thought I could make myself appear larger than life, someone people feared, like Morgan le Fay. It was childish."

"Morgan le Fay?"

"She was a goddess. A mythological character."

"You thought of yourself as a character in a legend."

"Yes."

"I know this is difficult—it's hard to talk about these things— but In the interest of telling the full story, I'd like to re-create the events of that day at the grocery store."

"That's what I'm here for." Lettie allowed something like

patience and understanding to inform her features. "Besides, it's not like I have anything left to lose."

COURTNEY BOWLES, TWO WEEKS AFTER ORN'S DISAPPEARANCE

Scud was halfway out the front door when Court came down the stairs demanding to know where he was going. She knew where—same place he went every day at this time—she just wanted to hear him say it. She needed to hear him say it. He wasn't supposed to leave the house without telling her where he was going, who he was seeing, when he was coming back. Those were the rules.

His head tilted back like he was pleading with the lord above, asking for patience, for the strength to deal with his mother's craziness. Or at least that's how Court saw it.

Exhaling loudly, Scud turned around, held up the bulky gym bag looped around his shoulder. Every day he was getting stronger, his shoulders broader, his head harder. Every day he was becoming more like his father.

"Mom, you know where I'm going." And then he was gone, the door slamming shut behind him, just as Court made her way to the bottom of the stairs. Just like that, in the time it took to walk down a flight of stairs, the sound of his voice still fresh, then fading, all too soon.

During the offseason, the football team had two practices a day, four days a week. Court knew this. She just wanted to hear him say where he was going. She wanted the reassurance of knowing when he would be home. That way, she didn't have to worry. But he couldn't even give her that much. He couldn't be bothered. He was giving her less and less lately, less information, fewer details, more obstinacy. He was spending more and more time out of the house, leaving earlier, coming home later. He threw himself into football. When he wasn't playing football he was hanging out with his friends at McDonald's. It kept him busy. The regularity of it all seemed to take his mind off things.

Court stood there at the bottom of the stairs, hand on the banister, absent-mindedly staring into space. She suddenly worried that Scud forgot his water bottle. It got so hot in the afternoon and he needed to stay hydrated. She'd heard stories of high school football players who dropped dead from heat exhaustion in the middle of practice, in the middle of the afternoon, dropped dead right there in front of their teammates. Sometimes Scud forgot his water bottle. He pushed himself so hard. He was so driven. There was always the possibility that he would push himself over the edge. There was always the possibility that he would just drop dead.

She went into the kitchen and searched for Scud's water bottle, making sure he hadn't left it behind. He could be so forgetful. She checked the dishwasher. She checked the cabinets—nothing. He must have taken it with him. That was good. It made her feel better. Still, she didn't know for sure, and sometimes not knowing was worse than knowing. This time, though, not knowing made her feel better.

Court hoped Scud would come straight home after practice.

He didn't want to spend time with his family. When he was home he stayed in his room and kept the door shut. She didn't blame him. There was so much pain in their house. His mom and dad were hurting. Everyone missed Orn. It was natural for Scud to try to avoid that pain. He was so young. He stayed away as much as he could. He locked himself away as much as he could. And when he did finally come home he was always starving. He never ate enough. He was still growing, nearly as big as his dad these days. Court opened the cupboards again, checked the fridge. They were low on food. She hadn't gone shopping in weeks. She hadn't gone shopping since that day, since Orn went—. Scud would be hungry when he got home. He wouldn't have an excuse to go to McDonald's after practice if there was food in the house.

She grabbed her purse, grabbed her keys. She backed the minivan out of the driveway, hit the brakes, turned the wheel.

The pills made it difficult to drive some days. Her hands felt like hard rubber. Sometimes they tingled. It was difficult to stay focused on the road. Sometimes she saw strange shapes haunting her periphery, human-sized blackbirds or weird shambling beasts. Other times she saw faces. She saw faces reflected in puddles, oily and rippling. She saw faces in the formations of electrical sockets. She saw them roiling in the dark—human faces, twisted up in pain, masks of agony—mouths opening up onto new faces, vomiting forth, blooming from within.

Dizziness, memory problems, trouble concentrating, anxiety, nausea—her doctor had warned her about these things when he gave her the pills. Take two of these a day, he said, avoiding eye contact. Take one in the morning and another at night, he said, tearing the prescription from its pad.

Court pulled into one of the empty spaces in the grocery store parking lot. She walked through the automatic sliding doors and grabbed a cart. Everything was so bright, the world in motion, lights buzzing in the high ceiling. She ignored all the people, everyone staring, the haunting faces. She knew people stared at her. She knew what they were thinking. There goes that poor woman, the one whose son went—. She grabbed anything she could think of, anything she thought Scud might want. She grabbed lunch meats and sliced cheese, eggs, boxes of cereal, two gallons of milk, cottage cheese, string cheese, plain yogurt, yogurt with fruit in it, yogurt that had fruit flavoring, cans of tuna fish, ground beef, ground chicken, ground turkey, jars of pickles, canned soups, canned salmon, canned ravioli, two loaves of white bread, English muffins, frozen pizzas, frozen meals, frozen French fries, ice cream, macaroni and cheese, spaghetti, spaghetti sauce, spaghetti in cans, potato chips, pitas, crackers, protein bars, breakfast bars, Gatorade, orange juice, bottled water, cans of Coke, root beer, Sprite, Dr. Pepper. It didn't matter what she grabbed. It didn't seem like nearly enough.

She saved the fruits and vegetables for last so they wouldn't get crushed beneath everything else in the cart. And when she was there, filling the little plastic bags with fruits and vegetables, the song "Singin' in the Rain" started playing from small speakers in the ceiling. The sprinklers came on, spraying the fruits and vegetables while the song played, a rainbow shimmering in the mist, the full spectrum of color suddenly visible, emerging from nothingness. It was so delicate, so ephemeral. It was as beautiful a sight as Court could imagine. Then she was weeping, quietly crying to herself. Then it was over. The song was over. Those beautiful colors disappeared. She was fine. She was okay. She just had to get home and get the groceries in the fridge and then she'd be good as new, she'd be right as rain.

That was when she saw him. Just as she left the fruits and vegetables section and before she made it to the checkout—that was when she saw Orn.

It wasn't the first time she'd seen Orn since he went—. Some nights she saw him standing still in the corner of her bedroom. She saw him standing along the side of the road as she drove past, his unblinking eyes tracking her movement. Always he stood perfectly still, hands at his sides, his mouth moving slightly as if speaking, as if he was trying to tell her something. This time was different though. This time Orn was covered with mud, his long hair soaking wet. His clothes were torn to shreds, hanging loose from his wiry limbs. Everything looked warped, the bones beneath his skin malformed. His skin was mottled, threaded with spidery dark blue veins. His eyes were milky white. When he opened his mouth a serpent-shaped stream of discolored water wriggled loose and thrashed against the floor.

Court covered her mouth with her hand, stifling a scream, the sound of it lodging in her throat. And then he was gone. As abruptly as he had appeared. The motion and the bright lights of the store surrounded Court once again. Orn was gone, and she'd never stopped moving, still pushing the cart from the fruits and vegetables section and toward the checkout.

Her doctor had never said anything about seeing visions of people who had gone—. He'd neglected to mention that when he'd given her the pills.

Orn was out there somewhere, scared and alone. He was still

out there, waiting to be found. Deep down in her heart, she'd never stop believing that. She couldn't. That would be the death of her. It made things harder when the police found Orn's Jeep, abandoned and blood stained. Then they said the blood type was a match. That made things harder still. Even then, she believed he was out there somewhere.

She slid into the nearest checkout aisle, pulling items out of the cart at random, tossing them onto the conveyor belt, doing all the things she was supposed to do in a grocery store. Right away she knew something was wrong. The checkout girl didn't say hello, didn't swipe the items over the scanner. Everything started piling up on the conveyor belt.

Court looked at the girl's face. She looked into her eyes. Then she saw the girl's nametag. And it was like everything stopped— the sound, the light, the movement. Court saw it in the girl's eyes, how scared she was. All her thoughts, her feelings, the things she wanted to say. They all piled up.

Lettie just stood there, wide eyed, wavering, unsure of what to do or what to say. Something blared over the store's loudspeakers, something Court couldn't understand, the bent, blaring sound of microphone feedback.

"I didn't know," the girl said.

"Didn't know what?" Court's voice was flat. She couldn't believe she was talking to the Underhill girl, Orn's supposed girlfriend, of all people, here in the grocery store checkout line. This tramp. This piece of Underhill trash.

"Any of it. I didn't know anything. I still don't."

"What the fuck are you talking about? What do you mean? You're the reason he's gone. You deserve to suffer for what you've done."

"I haven't done anything."

"You hurt him. I know you did. A mother knows."

Lettie's face twisted up with anger. "You're crazy."

"I'm crazy? I'm Orn's mother. Do you know what that means? Who are you?" And then, her voice low, "You're trash. You and your family—nothing but trash."

Lettie was really angry now. Her nostrils flared. Her eyes narrowed to two little slits. "You know what? Orn hates you. He always talks about how much he hates you. He told me that you suffocate him. He'd rather be dead than live another day in your house. Did you know—"

Before she even knew what she was doing, Court slapped Lettie across the mouth. She reached over the conveyor belt and slapped the girl in the mouth. Before she could stop herself. She saw the girl's lips part slightly, the gleam of her white teeth between flushed-red lips. Everything gleamed beneath the bright, buzzing lights.

That was when the world returned—the motion, the flow. Someone in line behind her gasped. A man working the next checkout line said something loudly, coming toward them. Court's whole body shook uncontrollably. She'd never been this angry before. She couldn't imagine that anyone could ever be this angry. Suddenly the store manager was there, a stocky man with a mustache. He was trying to restrain Court, who was trying to climb over the conveyor belt, flailing her arms, screaming. Someone else came and pulled Lettie away. The girl was crying.

Court held locks of Lettie's hair in her fists, their roots bloody, tiny clumps of skin shining in the light. She kept screaming until the lights of a police cruiser flashed blue and red through the store's front windows.

Two officers flanked Court, taking her by each arm, marching her to the cruiser, telling her that was enough, that she needed to calm down. Everyone was staring. The officers put Court in the back seat of the cruiser, slammed the door. "We're taking you home, Mrs. Bowles," one of them said. "You can pick up your car once you've had some rest."

She heard it in their voices, what they really thought. You're not well, Mrs. Bowles. You're fucking nuts, lady. You shouldn't be out here, you fucking crazy bitch. She heard her doctor's voice after he tore the prescription from its pad, "Take two of these a day, Mrs. Bowles. Try to forget you ever felt love in your heart." The awful tearing sound of the paper being ripped from its pad.

Court lay on her side in the back seat of the police cruiser. She couldn't stop crying. She was upset because she'd left all that food behind. Now Scud wouldn't have anything to eat when he came home from practice. He was always so hungry and there was no food in the house. He was still growing. All she wanted was for Scud to come home after practice so she'd know where he was. That way she wouldn't have to worry about him.

The cruiser slowed, stopped. The officers opened her door. Court was quiet then. She worried that she was in trouble. One of the officers helped her to her feet. Then he undid her handcuffs. She stood there in the driveway of her house, rubbing her wrists.

The sun was out. It was warm. It was such a beautiful day. Court had just a moment to register how strange it was to think that something could be so beautiful, yet remain so totally unaffected by its beauty.

Frank and Hunter were out on the porch, talking to a man

and a woman Court didn't recognize. The man and the woman stood there looking official, standing up straight, puffing out their chests. The woman wore a silk blouse tucked into pressed slacks, and the man wore a suit coat, slightly rumpled, as if he'd slept in it. Still rubbing her wrists, Court crossed the yard. The two officers followed closely behind, the sound of their heavy gear shifting.

It was the look on Frank's face that told her. It was the look on his face as she rushed to him. She'd seen that look on his face only once before, when Orn was still a baby, when he ran a fever of 102 and they'd taken him to the hospital. She and Frank were so young back then and they'd been so scared. They hadn't known what was wrong with their son. They drove Orn to the pediatric emergency room. That was when she'd seen the look on Frank's face. It was the look of not having the answers, of wondering what they could have done differently, of having let things go too far.

Frank's big arms closed around her, took her in, held her tight, a sensation that was both familiar and unfamiliar. Court no longer felt like herself. She heard herself crying but she didn't feel anything anymore. She was gone. Now she knew. She knew the truth and it destroyed her. She wished more than anything that she could go back to not knowing.

They went inside and Frank helped Court onto the couch. Hunter cleared away a bunch of trash. Frank sat next to Court and continued holding her. She smelled whiskey on his breath. He was drinking again. The thought of it made her sick to her stomach.

The two uniformed officers talked quietly to the man and the woman in the nice clothes for a while. Then one of them told Frank that he'd joined the force when Frank's dad was still the chief. They said Large Carl was a good man. They were going to cut Court a break. They knew things had been tough lately. "Tell Large Carl we're cutting Court a break," they said. Then they left. The man and the woman in the nice clothes stood opposite Frank and Court. They said they were detectives. They had been working on finding Orn. They had some bad news, as if that wasn't obvious enough.

That morning a fisherman found what they believed to be the body of Ornithan Bowles in a shallow cave along a remote stretch of Copper Creek. The cause of death was still being determined. For now, they needed a positive ID. There were other things they needed to discuss, the detectives said, but Court didn't need to worry about any of that right now. Right now they needed a positive ID. Right now Court needed to prepare for the worst. They asked Court if she would be all right. She said she would be fine. Frank held her tighter. She realized then that she was prepared for this. She had always been prepared for this.

Hunter spoke up from the kitchen doorway. He said he'd look after his sister. Then Frank volunteered to go to the medical examiner's office. He kissed Court on her forehead and left with the detectives. The front door shut behind them. He'd left her behind. He was so eager to get out of there. She could barely believe it. Was he fucking serious? Why the fuck had he kissed her on her forehead? Was she a child?

Her brother's voice came to her from a million miles away. "Do you need anything? Is there anything I can do?" And when she didn't respond right away he crossed the room and loomed over her. "Listen to me. I'm here for you. I need you to believe that."

Orn had always had it in his blood—whatever it was that made Hunter such a fuck-up. It was something Court had always worried about. They were similar in so many ways, Hunter and Orn. They were both so affected by everything, even the smallest little things. Ever since Hunter got parole and started sleeping on their couch, things with Orn had only gotten worse. She saw that clearly now. Hunter was a poison. She had let things go too far, for too long.

"I'm going upstairs to get some rest," she said, standing up from the couch. "By the time I wake up, I want you out of this house."

"Court, come on, I don't have anywhere to go."

She pushed past him, made her way to the stairs.

She shut the bathroom door behind her, made sure it was locked. Downstairs she heard Hunter slam the front door. Fuck him. She looked at her face in the mirror. Fuck you too.

If only she could return to not knowing. She opened the medicine cabinet and took down the small orange bottle of pills her doctor prescribed her. He'd handed her the prescription and said something like, "You might not feel like yourself some days, but these will help with the pain."

That was exactly what she wanted. She wanted nothing more than for the pain to go away.

Court popped the cap on the bottle and poured its contents into her mouth. God knew how many. She turned on the faucet, bent her head under the tap, and drank deeply. She choked it all down, all the pills, all the pain. Down the drain. She was tired of feeling like herself. She was so tired. Surely this would help her get some sleep. No more feeling like herself. She sat on the floor, her back against the tub, closed her eyes, and waited.

STEPHEN UNDERHILL, THE NEXT DAY

Columns of dusty sunlight slanted through Lettie's bedroom window. The air was sweltering, sweet, curling with clouds of silver smoke. One of Orn's self-recorded tapes hissed from the stereo, crackling with feedback, the occasional cluster of dissonant high notes.

Lettie lay face down on her mattress, arms and head hanging slack over the side. Stephen sat on the floor nearby. From his perspective it looked like his sister floated serenely in still water, doing the dead girl's float. He thought about how fucked up it was to think that as he took another hit from the small glass pipe, filling the resin-clogged chamber, releasing the shotgun, sucking down the stream of white smoke. He held it in his lungs and focused on the bliss expanding in his skull.

Why did weightlessness feel so good? It went beyond the absence of gravity, those invisible chains that tethered the body to the Earth. The euphoria of weightlessness was nothing less than a return to the womb, the warmth and comfort of amniotic fluid. It was the security of being in utero, unconscious, of belonging to something larger than yourself.

Stephen exhaled. He felt most like himself in this space, disembodied, an electric brain floating in oblivion, accepting that things would reveal themselves. Only then, given time, did his thoughts snap together in such satisfying, surprising ways—a drifting, cosmic puzzle.

Kate was sprawled out on her side at his feet, snoring lightly. He ran his hand over the dog's soft fur, stroked her side, then zoned out on Lettie's ball python, Syd, as she slithered soundlessly through the artificial vegetation in her terrarium. How fucking weird was it to live with animals? That some animals should come to accept humans as their guardians—their masters.

Orn's strange, menacing music thinned into razor-sharp tremolo riffing.

"Did he just record himself playing guitar all day long?"

"I can't believe he's actually dead," Lettie said, ignoring her brother. She spoke directly into the mattress, her voice muffled. Then she rolled over onto her back, folded her hands on her chest. She'd finally stopped crying. "I've been expecting him to turn up dead since the day I met him, and now that he's actually dead, it seems totally unreal."

Stephen passed Lettie the pipe and the lighter. She propped herself up on her elbow, took another hit, and made convulsive noises as she fought to hold in the smoke. She eventually burst out in a coughing fit, her face turning bright red.

Imagine not being able to breathe. Imagine drowning. Imagine knowing that you're going to die and having to live with this thought until your lungs fill with water, until your thoughts go black. You open up and you pull it in and that's it.

Just that morning the news spread that Orn's body had been

found in Copper Creek. Within a few hours it was like everyone knew. It was weird the way that worked, the way news spread so quickly from person to person, especially after something bad happened. People seemed to love bad news. They relished being the one to say that something horrible had happened to someone else, everyone thinking, hey, at least it wasn't me.

All the more reason to believe in pure consciousness, Stephen thought, a unified field of fundamental forces and elementary particles, a place where everything was born, where everything returned to die, and in doing so was born again. The primordial muck.

"Wherever Orn is," Stephen said, "he's in less pain than when he was alive." He saw the way Lettie looked at him, not grasping what he was trying to say. He was fucking it up. He wasn't saying what he meant. "I know you cared about him, but isn't it better this way?" He gestured to the stereo. "Now it's like he just exists in the music he made. He's like an energy, you know? I think he might have wanted it that way."

"No, I don't know," Lettie said, still coughing a little. She passed back the pipe. "Now that he's dead, it just seems like such a waste. All that time and energy he put into playing guitar, listening to music, figuring out all the parts. Why did he bother?" She went quiet for a moment. "He was always figuring out people too. He told me he saw parts of me that no one else did. Now, the parts of me that existed in Orn are all gone. I know this is going to make me sound selfish, but part of me misses him because of how I saw myself through him. He had his own version of me, and I liked that version of me best."

"That is very . . ." Stephen searched for exactly the right word, "depressing." He wasn't sure he'd understood what she was trying to say, not really. He was confused. Maybe she hadn't meant for it to be sad and he'd responded inappropriately. Or maybe she was just as fucked up as he was. He suddenly felt very anxious.

The cassette tape in the stereo stopped, flipped over, and started playing the other side. The tone was totally different, almost pleasant. A few slow, jangly notes looped once and then Orn's voice faded in, self-assured and astoundingly pretty. It took Stephen a moment to realize it was a cover of Love's "Alone Again Or."

It was one of Lettie's favorite songs. She buried her face in the mattress, placed both hands on the back of her head, elbows pointing straight ahead, and screamed.

There was so much distance between them. Whole gaps. Worlds of space. They had grown so far apart. And there was so much he needed to tell her. He'd been waiting for just the right moment, but the right moment never came. He wanted to close that distance and start all over again.

Stephen went to his room and came back with the glass eyedropper. Lettie looked up, saw what he had. "Oh, shit."

Kate seemed to know something was up. She sighed, climbed to her feet, and shuffled out of the room.

Lying flat on her back, Lettie pried open one eye with her thumb and her forefinger. "Shoot me right in my stupid brain."

Stephen released a single shuddering drop of the best acid he'd ever made—something new and beyond even his wildest expectations. Lettie's pupil went supernova. Stephen put the dropper in his mouth and closed his lips around it. He'd gotten so good at making this stuff so quickly. The only difficult part was obtaining the ergotamine, but it was doable as long as you knew the right people.

It didn't take long. He felt the sensation of pure acceleration, of being pushed back as he was propelled forward, pulled into outer space as the weight of his body remained tied to the Earth. A sound like an air-raid siren steadily rose in pitch, higher, higher still. Over and over again, winding and unwinding. Every breath was bliss. His anxiety left him, replaced by something else entirely.

The room got hazier, the sun brighter, the heat hotter. Orn's presence was there with them, sitting there on the bed playing the guitar, radiating an evil green aura, moving through warped and washed-out renditions of 60s folk and psychedelic rock. There he was, as if he'd never left. His eyes were milky white. Rivulets of water poured from his nose, his mouth.

Stephen wasn't scared. He felt no fear. If anything, he was comforted. He felt only love for Orn, accepted his spirit as an extension of his own being.

There was so much feeling in this music, so much intensity bubbling up around the edges, so much that went unsaid. Orn had made this music for Lettie, for Stephen's sister. Orn expressed something deep within himself every time he strummed the strings, with every chord, every word he sang. And only in thinking this did Stephen fathom what his sister had lost, like seeing light bend around an object in the dark, hinting at its true form, something impossibly large, impossibly empty. A hole in things.

He closed his eyes for what felt like an entire lifetime, adrift in an endless nothingness, and when he finally opened them he saw Lettie moving toward Syd's terrarium. She held a pair of metal tongs in one hand, a frozen feeder mouse in the other.

Her movements appeared in slow motion, the languid smoke perfectly curling in response, rushing to fill the vacuum of where she'd been. Through the window, the golden Sun formed a crown behind her head.

The snake's skin seemed to shine, each scale a brightly colored gem beneath the white-hot heat lamp, eyes like two swirling black holes. Reptile eyes. Cold and unfeeling. You enter that darkness, Stephen thought, and you never come out.

Lettie removed the lid of the terrarium, releasing the smell of rotting animal flesh. The smell was everywhere, maybe it always had been, but now it was impossible to ignore, the way it cut through the smoke, primal and prehistoric—the smell of the evil green aura.

Using the tongs, Lettie dangled the mouse from its tail a few inches from the snake. Syd focused on her prey, her body contorted in a series of tight, bow-shaped curls. She couldn't help but behave like the creature she was. She slithered forward impossibly slow. Then she struck, pulled the mouse from the tongs, and curled her body around it. She flexed, her skin shuddering from her head to her tail, gently swallowing the mouse bit by bit, opening and closing her distended jaw.

It was so beautiful. It was so purely animalistic, so unfeeling. There was no thinking. It was pure instinct that allowed the species to survive for more than a hundred million years, to proliferate during the Paleocene. Everything came down to survival. It was all so simple. The weakest were the most sensitive—people like Orn. They were prey with soft skin, exposed bellies, fleshy throats. Snakes felt nothing and thought nothing. They were cold and they were calculating and that was why they survived.

Stephen was reminded of how when astronauts in outer space saw the Earth in its entirety for the first time, when they saw it floating out there in outer space, they were overcome by the thought that it was little more than a fragile ball of life. Our giant, teeming world, all of humanity itself, its history, when seen from far enough away, was nothing more than a glowing orb, appearing delicate as glass.

Someday, some rock would come flying in from out of nowhere and decimate the entire thing, just blow it all to pieces. Those pieces would be propelled into space in a million different directions, all revolving around the black hole at the center of the galaxy, its spiral arms curling into oblivion, only to reform into something else, new matter, someday maybe even new planets crawling with new lifeforms. Things that had never been would come into existence, others would wink out in the dark. Everything else would go up in smoke, ghosts lurking in the periphery.

The lifeforce had awakened at the beginning of time in the farthest reaches of space, expanding and tumbling chaotically, puckering out perfect white orbs. Everything emerged from the lifeforce. It was an ocean of pure consciousness at the source of all thought and matter. Stephen knew it was out there because he'd ascended to new planes of existence, where the dead walked among the living, where shadows breathed and light had its own language.

"I can feel the planet dying," he said. "It's been crying out but no one can hear it. It's our fault everything is dying. We just can't stop crawling all over it."

"I wish I could leave it all behind." Lettie's voice shook. She opened and closed her fists, standing there watching the snake still choking down the mouse. "None of this is even real. It's like . . . holograms. Two-dimensional holograms frozen in time at the rim of a black hole."

"Oh, shit, you don't even know how right you are."

Stephen's line of sight framed Lettie in the light of the bedroom window, the setting sun now blazing orange in the rippled, purple sky. The clouds were slipping sideways. The colors were apocalyptic, bleeding into one another, breathing, each heartbeat a thunderous force.

It was like she knew what he was thinking—one of those electric moments of theirs. She turned to the window and raised her arms, fingers extended, palms turned inward. She held her hands on either side of the black sun, patiently cradling its descent, as if laying it to rest.

With enough power, a person could guide the old world into its eternal slumber, reach deep into the glistening black pool, and unveil the new dawn. A new era with new kinds of snakes, things that did what had to be done to survive, to evolve.

"You and I came into the world together," she said, speaking even though her mouth was not moving. "We are the same—two parts of a whole."

Stephen saw his face where hers should have been. He felt her heart where his should have been. They were hatched from the same egg. And as one, he explained to her that he had come to realize certain things about who they were, about the blood they had flowing through their veins. The distance between them was an illusion. The separations between living things were meant to corral people into dead ends, send them climbing up staircases that went nowhere. Time and space had no limits. Everything was flat.

There were no rules. Not if your mind was free.

Together, the two of them could leave this world. They simply had to ascend high enough to kick away the bloated, gaseous carcass of the old world beneath their feet, turn through space at just the right angle, and land where they wanted to be.

They would be free—as one.

Orn's screeching guitar reached a crescendo.

The light of the world collapsed into a line on the horizon. The sky went dead. Annihilation was imminent.

Later that night, when they were both coming down, Lettie and Stephen climbed out her bedroom window and onto the roof of the old house. They sat beneath the stars, the nighttime sky rippling like a pale ocean, and they smoked cigarette after cigarette, talking rapidly about anything and everything that popped into their heads, sharing their deepest emotions, their darkest fears, and ultimately feeling closer than they had since they were children. After some time, they fell into contemplative silence.

"I'm really sorry," Stephen said. "About everything."

"I know." Lettie swept her arm from side to side, gesturing to the world below. "All of this—this is all we have left. We need to stay strong for each other."

"Yeah." Stephen flicked a cigarette butt over the edge of the roof, watched its glowing orange tip turn end over end and out of sight.

"Earlier tonight, when we were just coming up, I felt Orn's presence. I know you did too. He was there and he was playing his music. That part of him is still out there—the pure part. His spirit or whatever. It's like you said earlier, he still exists in his music. The energy that he created when he was alive still lingers, just waiting for us to feel it, you know? It's like people can leave their mark on something and never leave your life."

A shooting star streaked a white line across the sky, just a flash, and then it was gone.

"Did you see that?" Letting pointed to the sky. "Oh, wow. That was the first shooting star I've ever seen."

She was smiling. She was happy again, at least for now.

The time had come. He told her how he had followed her and their grandmother out into the woods a few weeks back, the night after Orn disappeared, and that he heard the things their grandmother said, about their parents' deaths, about who was responsible.

He told her how he went into town the next day and went through the public records at the library, how he spent hours digging through files, day after day, digging through newspaper articles and official documents and certificates. He told her he was obsessed with knowing more, with discovering who he was, where he came from, what it all meant.

It was true that their family had been in Stone River since the beginning, just like their grandmother always said, but the Bowles family had been in Stone River for just as long. He'd never really believed the rumors of a feud between the two families, thinking it was nothing more than a local legend.

Except the feud was real, and many people on both sides had died because of it. He told her he had found articles dating back more than a hundred years that chronicled the two families killing each other. The names of the dead added up to nearly forty people, all of them distant cousins, once, twice removed, people who had married in, people who had been in the wrong places at the wrong times. There were instances of arson and robbery, lynching and rape, bludgeoning and swindling. And all of it could be traced back to when their family still owned and operated the coal mine.

"Jesus Christ. I had no idea."

"Wait. It gets weirder."

House Underhill was built right on top of those mines, but there was more to it than that. A network of stone tunnels formed a labyrinth. Some of those tunnels were bricked over, just like their grandmother said. Others were flooded. He'd been going down there at night with only a flashlight, seeing where they went, following the distant sounds of flowing water. The deepest tunnels connected to the mine shafts.

"I found a stone chamber down there. It feels as if the room itself is charged with an immense power—something bigger than us. Something evil. I don't know. It's hard to explain. The thing that we tap into when we connect, it's down there and it's even stronger." He paused. "Do you ever get the sense that there are restless spirits trapped below our house?"

Lettie said nothing. She didn't have to. He knew she did.

"I think they have something to do with that chamber. They're part of it somehow. Trapped there. Like something terrible happened and our house is a tomb."

Lettie scoffed, but then she saw he was being serious, that he meant what he said.

"Whatever we are, the answer is down there in those tunnels. And it's got something to do with this." He spread his palm over his forehead then placed his other hand over Lettie's forehead. They sat like that for several long moments, feeling the connection.

He removed his hand from her forehead. They looked at each

other. "We need to go down there together and open our eyes, connect with the plane of the dead, and see what reveals itself. Maybe we can even set it free."

HUNTER HOLBROOK, THE NEXT DAY

Hunter unscrewed the cap on the bottle of Jack Daniel's, stared down its neck, and breathed in the great, sour smell of it. He screwed the cap back on, put the bottle on the nightstand next to the bed. A rebroadcast of yesterday's White Sox–Royals game played on the shitty TV. He tried to focus on the game, watched a couple pitches. The images on the screen looked washed out, warped. He looked at the bottle, just sitting there on the nightstand, the way the light from the wall-mounted lamp filtered through the rich amber-colored liquid. Fuck it. He picked it up, unscrewed the cap, and took a long swig. It went down easy. A moment later he took another swig.

He'd spent so many days and nights in this room—some of the best moments of his life. With her. The love of his life. Now, he was alone.

Even with the blinds closed, the light in the room went weird. Hunter heard heavy rain falling against the motel's low, flat roof. His head buzzed. He smoked a cigarette lying in bed, tapping the ashes onto the carpet. Three innings went by before he heard the knock at the door.

He kept the chain on. Scud stood there, looking pissed off. Rain streamed from the ratty roof overhang. The sky was colorless. Hunter undid the chain and let Scud into the room, redid the deadbolt, the chain. Then he pulled back the blinds and scanned the parking lot. He saw Court's van. Nothing else out of the ordinary.

"It smells like something died in here," Scud said. He sat on the edge of the bed and leaned forward with his elbows on his knees, watching the game. Konerko swung and missed—strike three. Scud sucked air through his teeth. The game went to commercials.

Hunter dropped into the cheap armchair and lit another cigarette. "How's she doing?"

Scud shrugged, eyes still on the TV. "She's not saying much."

"Your dad?"

"Off the wagon." Scud sighed deeply. "He wants to know where you've been, obviously."

Hunter didn't say anything. They sat there for a while, letting the commercials play out. There was one for tires, another one for a chain of grocery stores.

"I found her, you know," Scud said. "When I got back from football practice. Her car wasn't there but the bathroom door was locked. I heard the faucet running. I told her I was home but she didn't respond. Somehow I just knew. I kicked the fucking door down and called 911."

Hunter smoked his cigarette slowly. Never, not in a million years, did he think Court would hurt herself. He never would have left her alone if he'd thought that. She still had a son to look after, as strange as it was to think of it that way.

"Listen," Hunter said, or started to say. He didn't know what to say after that. "No way Konerko is worth the $37 million."

You did what I couldn't, he thought. Still just a kid. You were there when I wasn't.

Scud stood up and turned off the TV. The commercials zipped into a small blue dot at the center of the screen before disappearing altogether. "We should go. Besides, Sox lost this one four to seven."

The minivan's windshield wipers squeaked back and forth, sticking slightly. Scud had the AC cranked and the windows up. Alice in Chains played on the radio, then Metallica, then Tool. Hunter cracked his window, let the rain soak the inside of the door. He smoked cigarette after cigarette even though he knew he wasn't supposed to smoke in Court's car. Fuck, how could she have been so selfish?

Scud filled Hunter in on everything that had gone down. Orn's official cause of death was drowning—water in his lungs. And even though they weren't supposed to, the cops told Large Carl they were treating the case as a homicide. Orn's forearm was all cut up, but they wouldn't say how badly. They found drugs on him, too, but they wouldn't say what kind or how much. All part of an ongoing investigation, they said.

Hunter stared straight ahead, processing everything. All of his worst fears were confirmed. Orn had gotten in too deep and it was all his fault. He reached down and grabbed the bottle of whiskey from between his feet, took another quick nip. It wasn't helping much. There was no getting around what he had to do, the conversation he had to have with Frank, the dread he felt rising up inside him as fiery and bitter as bile. He'd waited too long. Fucking idiot. Why hadn't he just said something when he first had the chance? Too chickenshit. He got the cap back on the bottle just as he caught the shape of the cop cruiser swinging out onto the road, its headlights shining in the rain.

Scud turned off the commercial strip and entered the shitty part of town, out near the old cemetery. The cop followed. The stoplight ahead turned yellow.

Hunter grabbed Scud's forearm and squeezed. "Run the light. Do it."

"The fuck?" Scud wrenched his arm free. The van jerked slightly. He'd already hit the brakes, was already slowing, coming to a halt. The cruiser stopped behind them.

Hunter put his cigarette out in the dash ashtray, rolled up his window.

"Listen, I missed a parole appointment. I've been waiting for them to show up and take me in." He turned and looked Scud in the eye. "I'm not being paranoid. If they make me drop I'll piss dirty. I need you guys to hide me out. I can't go back to prison, man. As long as I live I won't go back there."

Scud rubbed his forearm. "Running the light would just draw more attention to us." He was weirdly calm. The look on his face was a combination of pity and disgust. "Did that not occur to you?"

Hunter looked away. It hadn't. He was so fucking dumb sometimes, never thinking ahead, always panicking. Christ, his hands were shaking, he was so scared. The booze wasn't helping the way it usually did. A few seemingly endless moments later the light turned green.

The cop followed close behind, switched lanes every time Scud did, headlights burning holes in the rearview. Hunter's heart was pounding. The cop was probably running the minivan's plates right that moment. They knew he was Court's brother, that he listed her address as his place of residence. Any moment now and those blue and red flashers would come on and that would be that. He saw himself putting the barrel of a .45 in his mouth and pulling the trigger—saw it again and again, the image repeating on a loop. It calmed his nerves, knowing he could always end it if he had to.

Scud put on his signal, spun the wheel, and Hunter saw the cruiser glide by as the minivan turned onto the road that led to the hospital. The window was back down before he knew it, a cigarette lit. He must have killed the whole thing in five drags.

They parked the car, went inside, and took the elevator to Court's floor. The nurse at reception directed them to a small waiting room down the hall.

Large Carl and Frank were already there, both sitting with their arms crossed, an empty chair between them. Carl took his time getting to his feet. His silver beard was trimmed tight, complexion a deep red. He stood a full head taller than Hunter and nearly twice as wide. They shook hands, the old man nearly crushing every bone. Frank stayed put, his eyes hidden behind aviators. Hunter could smell the booze on Frank a mile away. He flashed the bottle in his coat. That earned him a nod of recognition.

Scud came around with paper cups half-filled with black coffee. Hunter topped them off. The four of them sat there in that tiny waiting room, sipping their coffees, the wall-mounted TV blaring a shitty sitcom. After a while, Hunter asked when he could see Court.

"No one's stopping you," Frank said.

Scud gave Hunter the room number, his eyes glued to the TV. Carl didn't say shit.

Hunter left the bottle with Frank. Then he shuffled down the hall, lights buzzing in the ceiling, the occasional nurse fast-walking past him in silent sneakers. He came to Court's door. The room was smaller than he expected it to be, cluttered with machines and cords. She was propped up at an angle in bed, her wrists tethered to the bed rails with black bands and foam bracelets. An IV drip was taped just above her elbow.

"That you, Hunter?" Her voice was gluey from whatever meds they had her on. Her eyelids looked heavy, purple and swollen.

"Hey. Just dropped in to see how you're holding up."

"Is Frank still here?" She closed her eyes, turned her head away ever so slightly.

"He's down the hall." Hunter ran his hand through his hair, scratched at his scalp. He desperately wanted to smoke. He didn't know what to say. Court decided for him.

"I don't want you blaming yourself for what happened."

The thought had never occurred to him, and the fact that she thought it would made him want to punch the fucking wall. "Why the fuck would I do that? You did this to yourself."

Court turned to him. "Jesus, you are such a fucking asshole," she said through clenched teeth.

"Oh, here we go."

"Ever since we were kids, you've been nothing but a selfish prick. I've been—"

"Again with the same shit."

"—bailing you out of one jam after another and never so much as a thank you, I'm sorry I'm such a fucking piece of poisonous shit."

Neither of them had it in them. Their bickering died down as quickly as it had begun. They'd done this routine a thousand times. Hunter thought maybe it was the only way they knew how to talk to each other, sad as that was. One of the machines next to Court's bed chirped.

He saw now that she was crying. How she looked ten years older than he remembered. He saw the lines of their mother's face in her features. He saw Orn's face in hers. He didn't think, just reached out and held her hand. Her fingers immediately closed over his.

"I've been seeing him. My boy. He's been coming to me in visions, trying to tell me something. Trying to warn us. Something is wrong. He's trapped between two worlds, somewhere out there. He's trapped and he's all alone."

Was it the drugs talking? Hunter couldn't be sure. Her grip on his hand suddenly tightened.

"The bad blood has awoken. I feel it in my bones. Don't you?"

"Court—"

"Shut the fuck up and listen to me. Just listen for once in your goddamn life. There's things I need to tell you while I can. You, me, and Frank. We're weaker when we keep to ourselves, when we're alone. That's how they got to Orn. He was all alone. We left him all alone. And now we need to be strong for what's to come." She paused. "It was that thing with Sweet Lou. That's what this is all about. Orn's death was retribution."

This was the last thing Hunter expected to hear Court say. Sweet Lou's name twisted through his mind like the blackest nightmare. All the grief, the self-loathing, the hatred, it all came rushing up and through him in an instant—the thing he hoped most to forget.

He remembered back when they were all kids, him and Frank Bowles and Peter "Saint Pete" Peters, the three of them thick as thieves. He was in love with Lucretia Underhill even then, had loved her ever since he could remember, the girl with the prettiest snaggletooth smile in the whole wide world—Sweet Lou. Then, in their junior year of high school, Hunter's little sister had taken up with Frank. Hunter and Saint Pete both made a move for Sweet Lou, but there was no way she'd date someone whose sister was with a Bowles, at least that's what she told Hunter one night, angled over the bright green pool table in the back of the Pop-a-Top, an unlit cigarette dangling from her lips. She stretched out one of her pale, thin arms, sleeves of her white T-shirt rolled up over her bare shoulder, and slammed the eight ball into the corner pocket.

Hunter had never gotten over it. His one true love. The love of his life. He'd never gotten over it and she'd never really let him, meeting him every couple months in that ratty motel outside of town, the same room Hunter had been hiding in the past two days, the room in which he'd spent the best days of his miserable, shitty life.

And then one night almost exactly thirteen years ago, drunk out of his mind, fucked up on Percocet, he got into his car and drove off into the night. He woke up in the hospital two weeks later with a collapsed lung and a fractured femur bone, charged with two counts of vehicular homicide.

How he'd ever come into contact with Saint Pete's car that night was utterly beyond him. What were the odds? How the fuck do you explain that? It was almost like he'd been destined to kill her. That was his punishment, knowing that he'd killed her. If only he could find a way to set it right, he would. He wouldn't think twice.

There was a knock at the door. A nurse came in and said it was time for Court to take her meds. She told Hunter that visiting hours were over soon. He barely heard what she said, mumbling his goodbyes to his sister. She held his hand so tight. She wouldn't let go. He finally pulled free.

Scud was gone when he got back to the waiting room. Carl stood as Hunter approached. "The boy said you're in some kind of trouble? That you need to get out of sight for a while?"

Hunter nodded.

"All right then. You're coming with us."

The three of them—Large Carl, Frank, and Hunter—piled into the old man's massive F-350. They tore through town and out onto the old backroads. The Moon was full, a pink disc hovering in the purple-bruised night. Willie's *Stardust* played on the stereo.

They curved around a long dirt drive that led to one of the old man's newly built houses. The surrounding property had been cleared of trees, the yard unplanted, and these things together gave the house a foreboding, skeletal quality. The crew had just wrapped up a few days ago. It wouldn't be comfortable, but Hunter could camp out here for a few days. They'd have to bring him food and water, an electric lamp, a sleeping bag, some books and magazines. He'd have to shit in the woods.

It was totally empty inside, no furniture, no carpet, no socket wall plates, no nothing. Sound carried everywhere, sharp as knives. The windows still had the stickers and plastic bags glued to them. Everything was so new. The air smelled so clean, so sharp. Carl turned on the lights in the kitchen, which led out to the deck overlooking the sloping, woodsy backyard. The placid, still water of the lake rippled with the reflection of the Moon.

They stood around the granite-topped island, the bottle of Jack Daniel's, now nearly half-empty, at its center. None of them were particularly good at talking to one another. They didn't bother trying to be good at it. None of them cared about that. Instead, they drank, sliding the bottle across the counter to one another, taking turns taking pulls.

Finally, Carl said, "You gonna tell us what's going on with you?"

Hunter hadn't been planning on it. He didn't think he'd be able to find the right words. But the booze had loosened his tongue, given him enough courage, enough hope, to believe that maybe talking would do some good. And so he explained what Court told him about Lou, about how the bad blood was awake, or whatever it was she'd said.

Carl sighed loudly as he took another pull, this one maybe just a little longer than usual. "I always knew this day would come." He put his hand on Frank's shoulder but kept his eyes on Hunter. "I'd do anything for family. It doesn't matter to me. The law is one thing, but blood is blood."

Hunter was confused. "What do you mean?"

"It wasn't just Lou and Saint Pete who died that night."

Frank turned away. Hunter had the sudden sensation of waking from an unpleasant dream and becoming aware of an even more unpleasant reality.

"She was pregnant," Carl said, his voice low. "Lucretia Underhill. The night of the accident, she was maybe three or four weeks along. I know this isn't easy for you to hear, but it's the truth. When the autopsy results came back, I had them destroyed. As far as the official record was concerned, she'd never been with child. The medical examiner owed me a dozen favors—he was a man of many vices—so it was easy enough. Listen to me, the poor girl's family never even knew. I don't even think she knew yet. No one raised a fuss. It might as well have never been."

"Jesus Christ, man. Oh, fuck."

"I'm sorry. You weren't ever supposed to know. No one was. It wasn't anything that anyone needed to know, so far as I was concerned."

Hunter rushed to the sink and puked, nothing but whiskey and bile, stripping his throat raw. He felt the blood vessels burst around his eyes. It seemed like it was never going to stop, an ever-flowing stream. He wiped his nose and mouth on the sleeve of his shirt.

Carl and Frank gave him a moment to get it together.

When Hunter got back to the island, Carl pushed the bottle his way. Hunter took another swig, steeled his nerves.

"Why are you telling me now?"

"It's the right time," Carl said. "Time to act. Time to get everything out in the open. This thing with Orn changes everything. No more secrets."

Carl was right. Hunter knew that. Just like Court said, they were stronger when they talked to each other.

"There's something you both gotta know too. I couldn't say nothing before because Court was so fucking mad at first. I mean, I wanted to say something that morning. But I just thought Orn would show up on his own. Then another day went by. Then a whole week. Then it was too late."

"Spit it out," Frank said. "Goddammit, what are you trying to say?"

"Orn was dealing."

"Drugs?" Frank said. "Orn was dealing drugs? Are you fucking serious?"

"Just some weed, strips of acid—nothing serious."

Frank was on top of him in no time, swinging hard. Hunter tried to get his hands up but he was too slow. Frank's fist hit the side of his neck, then another landed on his shoulder. They tangled, hugging like tired boxers. Neither of them had it in them to fight. They just stood there, slow dancing, Frank swaying slightly from side to side, holding each other.

"You girls done?" Carl said.

"Listen," Hunter said, pulling away from Frank. "I'm not proud of any of this."

Frank leaned against the counter, eyes on the floor. He was beside himself.

"I found out through some guys I know. Orn wasn't so good about keeping a low profile. So I told him he needed to let me help him move some stuff. I was desperate for money, man. Court kept saying I had to chip in or I'd be out on my ass. She kept telling me I needed to get a job, but no one would hire me. Orn was pissed at me at first, but then he agreed."

"Jesus Christ, Hunter," Frank said. "This is low. Even for you."

"Wait. Just listen. This is important. A lot of people started asking me for more acid. They said it was the best they'd ever done. Like, world-class stuff. So I go back to Orn and I'm pumping him for information. And that's when Orn told me Stephen Underhill was the one who made the stuff in one of the old mining outposts. Think about it, man. Stephen fucking Underhill. One day Orn tells me this bit of privileged information and the next day he goes missing. That's gotta mean something, don't it?"

Carl reached for the bottle, took it from Hunter, took another pull, then handed it off to Frank, who did the same. Then it was

Hunter's turn. There was less than a finger left. Hunter killed it.

"We should see what the Underhill boy knows," Carl said. He reached behind his back and pulled out a snub-nose .38, pressed it to the countertop, next to the empty bottle of whiskey. The piece gleamed in the light. "What do you think? You boys up for paying him a visit?"

A HOTEL ROOM BY THE HIGHWAY

Lettie had the room's full attention. She could feel it. The air was still, silent. This was what everyone had been waiting for, building up to the big night. All anyone ever cared about was the part of the story where people got killed.

"People think they know what happened that night," she said, "but the story got twisted by the media. In fact, the so-called feud of the two families has always been twisted."

"What do you mean by that?" Barbara said.

"I mean that Stephen and I grew up hearing all these stories about how the Underhills and the Bowles hated each other. The so-called Hatfield and McCoys of Illinois. So that's what we believed. We believed it because other people believed it. But when I was with Orn, I never thought about any of that stuff. I loved him for who he was. Then, when his mom confronted me, I started thinking otherwise."

"And then Orn's father, grandfather, and uncle showed up at your house in the middle of the night?"

"That's right. They came to our home and they threatened us." Lettie softened her eyes. This was also something she'd practiced—

how to simultaneously convey recollection, fear, regret, anger. "They brought guns. You can't imagine how scared we all were."

"A moment ago you said the media twisted the story. What did they get wrong?"

"For starters, the idea that Stephen had anything at all to do with Orn's death. That simply wasn't—and isn't—the truth. Or the idea that we somehow deserved it. There was this narrative that we were backwoods people who practiced black magic, that we'd been cast out by society. The media helped perpetuate that narrative. They painted us as evil because we were poor."

"On that point, let's talk about some of the things you said during the trial."

Lettie sighed. "I knew we'd get to this eventually."

The tone of Barbara's voice sharpened. "Well, it's certainly important. Perhaps it is even the primary reason your story reached so many people—all those sensational headlines."

"I don't doubt that."

There was a brief pause. Barbara scrutinized Lettie's face. Lettie couldn't tell how much of this was the rhythm of the interview, doing the dance, performing for the cameras, and how much was Barbara seeking to assert control. The uncertainty made Lettie nervous. Still, she could not let her guard down. She could not show them that she was anything other than confident.

Lettie cracked first. "You're going to ask what everyone wants to know—about when I took the stand, even though my lawyers advised me not to. When I said I was the descendent of a long line of witches. Or when I said that the wrong done to my family would result in a curse on the Bowles family until every last one of them was dead and buried."

Barbara nodded, her face perfectly impassive. Lettie had fallen right into her trap and now it was too late to go back.

"It's just like the feud between the families. It was a common myth, but one we all bought into. Part of me really did think I was the descendent of witches because that was what I'd been told. My grandmother filled my head with stories, but they were just fantasy. When I was in school, all the other girls called me a witch. Their mothers wouldn't let them play with me. No one talked to me. So I believed what they said. It was even a bit of a joke in our family. Our dogs were named Hecate and Minerva—Kate and Minnie."

"You're saying that your family never practiced witchcraft?"

Lettie laughed. "Of course not. How can you practice something that doesn't exist?"

"And the case presented by the prosecutors—"

"More lies." Lettie waved away the question. "You've heard of the West Memphis Three? I'm no more a witch than those poor boys were Satanic child murderers. The prosecutors exploited people's superstitions to turn them against me. I don't blame them for that. They were just doing their jobs. I only wish I hadn't made it so easy for them." She shifted in her seat. "We weren't much different from every other family in America. In the early days of our town, my family had a lot of money. We helped build things. We gave a lot of people jobs. But when I was growing up, we struggled just like everyone else. We weren't rich. Our house was falling apart. Still, it's hard to escape the impressions people have of you once they're locked in, you know?"

Barbara continued nodding, perhaps a bit more sympathetically.

"That's how small-town stories get started. People talked about my family because everyone knew our name. Sure, I poured fuel on the fire during the trial. But I was young. I was scared. I thought maybe it would help me, as confused as I was."

Lettie remembered sitting there in that uncomfortable swivel desk chair, the black-robed judge looming over her, dignified and silver-haired, eyes inscrutable behind her thick glasses. She remembered the restlessness of the courtroom. Nearly everyone in the public seats seemed to be reporters, furiously scribbling notes. Back then, cameras weren't allowed in courtrooms. The atmosphere was suffocating, the eerie quiet interrupted by the occasional cough, the noise of shuffling papers, the moaning of the old wooden benches.

She closed her eyes—seeing it all again—and felt the heat of the box lights on her face. Her anger flared. This is how it must have felt, to be one of those misunderstood women burned at the stake. One of the countless women sacrificed to the ignorance of the masses, the women whose names went unspoken. Everyone always judging, pointing their fingers. To feel their eyes crawling all over you. This is what it felt like to be eaten alive by rage, always and forever unheard.

These people would never understand. They were idiots. She had to give them a version of the story that made sense to them.

"Are you comfortable talking about your time in prison?"

"I'd really rather not."

"I know you've only recently been released," Barbara said, not missing a beat. "But I feel like it's relevant. Don't you agree? We're here to clear the air, right?" She quickly flipped through a few of the papers in her lap. "Four years ago, It was reported that you had a romantic relationship with one of the corrections officers assigned to your pod, a woman named Shannon Bell. She was later sentenced for smuggling contraband into the prison, allegedly at your direction."

Lettie's anger was rising again. "Allegedly."

"According to the reports, Ms. Bell was smuggling in large amounts of liquid LSD—much of which was discovered in your cell—a plastic eyedrop bottle hidden in a hole carved in your wall."

"Drugs may have been discovered in my cell, but that doesn't mean they belonged to me."

"Fair enough. I'm not here to point fingers. But you've openly admitted to regularly taking hallucinogenic drugs with your brother, who formerly produced and distributed them. By your admission, you and Stephen were consuming large quantities of LSD in the months leading up to your incarceration."

"Prison is a miserable place. You're stuck in confined spaces. Your schedule is dictated for you. It's perfectly natural to want to escape reality any way you can. LSD is great for that. You hear all kinds of stories about people in prison taking heroin or smoking marijuana or making alcohol, but some people are looking for a more liberating experience. It's good to escape, even if it's just deeper into your own mind. I would sometimes take LSD in my cell at night, sure. It brought me back to myself. It reminded me that someday I would be free, that the concrete walls around me were not permanent. Is that so bad? It didn't hurt anyone."

Barbara went for the kill. "Truthfully, it seems like a lot of people in your life end up getting hurt."

Lettie looked to the crew, reading their reactions. She saw Mark in the back of the room, saw the pain on his face, and knew that she had his support. In that moment, it was everything and all that she needed.

"When it comes to my family," Lettie said, trying to speak levelly, "the people I loved, we were all just unlucky. Me, my brother, and especially Orn. Carl and Frank Bowles and Hunter Holbrook were all grown men. They should have known better."

"And what about Courtney Bowles?"

Lettie went cold. She didn't know what to say. Barbara seemed to sense this. She seemed to understand that it was too early, that she'd overplayed her hand. She quickly changed subjects.

"Let's revisit the night of the so-called massacre in more detail, yes? The version of events you related during your trial has been the focus of much coverage."

"Like I said, all of that is just make-believe."

"So, what did happen that night?"

"Exactly what was first reported. Carlton Bowles, Franklyn Bowles, and Hunter Holbrook showed up at our house in the early-morning hours. They brought guns. They tried to intimidate us. They threatened us. We fought back. And everything that happened that night—everyone who died—is a direct result of their actions and their choices. The facts speak for themselves."

THE HOUSE UNDERHILL MASSACRE

On Monday, June 28th, 1999, Carlton Bowles, his son Franklyn Bowles, and Franklyn's brother-in-law, Hunter Holbrook, climbed into Carlton's 1997 Ford F-350 and left the newly constructed house at Ash Tree Lake. They made one stop at an undisclosed location where they retrieved a Browning ten-gauge pump-action shotgun, one pair of thirty-six-inch bolt cutters, three five-gallon gas cans, one claw hammer, one thirty-six inch slotted-claw ripping bar, two bottles of Jack Daniel's whiskey, and one police-issue Taser X26 stun gun.

It was the night of the full moon, an otherwise quiet, uneventful evening. Eyewitness evidence was used to piece together the movements of the three men. First, Carlton Bowles's truck was spotted heading south from Ash Tree Lake toward Stone River. There, the three men stopped at a gas station. Security footage shows Hunter Holbrook pumped gas while Carlton and Frank Bowles purchased three bottles of Coca-Cola and three pieces of individually wrapped beef jerky. Hunter Holbrook then purchased a pack of Marlboro Red cigarettes. Fifteen minutes later, the F-350 was again spotted as the men traveled west through town and stopped at the residence of Franklyn and Courtney Bowles. Later testimony confirmed that Franklyn Bowles briefly spoke with his sixteen-year-old son, Scott. Franklyn told the boy, among other things, that he would need to look after his mother, Courtney Bowles, if anything bad happened. Forty-five minutes later, the F-350 was spotted for the last time that night as it crossed the covered bridge over Copper Creek and entered the deep woods surrounding House Underhill.

From there, the men had to stop at two security gates, spaced nearly a mile apart, along the winding drive that led to the house. Half-inch stainless steel chains were found in the road at both gates. It can only be assumed that the padlocks were broken using the bolt cutters. Tire tracks in the mud at both scenes matched the treads on the F-350 belonging to Carlton Bowles. An empty bottle of Jack Daniel's was also found in the woods some thirty yards after the second gate. A cigarette butt recovered in the road matched Hunter Holbrook's preferred brand.

The F-350 was found parked beneath an oak tree some fifty yards from House Underhill's front entrance. A single gas can was found unopened near the truck's rear wheels. The other two were never recovered and can only be presumed lost.

While the exact events of the House Underhill Massacre are still unknown, a general timeline was established during the trial of Letitia Underhill. It should be noted here that Letitia Underhill has expressed dissatisfaction with the official record on numerous occasions, stating each time that it did not account for important contextual detail. However, according to law enforcement, her numerous attempts to provide such detail or to correct the official record were deemed insufficient, misleading, or demonstrably false. In fact, during Ms. Underhill's appeal in 2005, prosecutors threatened to charge her with giving false testimony. Only then did she revise her story, offering instead a fact-based sequence of events. This revised testimony has remained consistent in subsequent years. As a result, what really happened on the night of the full moon remains a matter of speculation.

CARLTON BOWLES

The F-350's brakes squeaked as it came to a stop. Large Carl put it in park, killed the engine. The three of them sat there in shared silence, the exhaust system ticking like a heartbeat as it cooled in the nighttime air.

All these years and Carl had never once been so close to House Underhill. There was an unspoken rule among cops in Stone River: the Underhill property was off limits. It had always been that way. God knew why, a holdover from another era, maybe. The family kept to themselves, and in return, they were left alone. Yet, here he was all the same, mere steps from their front door.

The house was both bigger and dingier than he would have expected. Decades of neglect had stripped the siding, exposing weathered grey wood. The windows sagged. And creeping trees encroached from all sides, nature rising to reclaim a rightful belonging.

Hunter sucked on a cigarette in the backseat, blowing the smoke out the open window. Carl cracked open the third—and last—bottle of whiskey and handed it to him.

The windows of the house were dark. It was quiet.

"You think anyone's home?" Frank leaned his head against the passenger-side window to get a better angle.

The Underhills were home all right. They had to be. These people had nowhere else to go. They were in there, hiding in the shadows, watching. Carl could feel them. He knew they could feel him too.

That was fine by him. He wanted them to know he was here.

"We shouldn't be here, man," Hunter said. He took a pull of whiskey. "This is a bad idea."

Frank looked over his shoulder. "You're the voice of reason all of a sudden?"

How much easier things would have been, Carl thought, if only he'd let Hunter Holbrook rot in prison all those years ago. Things probably would have turned out better for everyone. That was the truth. And the truth always has a way of asserting itself, rising to the surface like earthworms after the rain.

"No more arguing, the both of you. We need to stay calm."

As much as he hated to admit it, Hunter was right. This was a bad idea. But they had no choice. Things had gone too far. These people had messed with his family. He couldn't let that stand.

"We owe it to Orn," Carl said. "It's the least we can do."

He had no idea what they were getting themselves into, not if he was being honest. Orn was dead. Nothing would change that. Court and Frank would have to live with that for the rest of their lives. It was unimaginable, that sort of pain. Their first-born son. And there was more yet left to lose. Scud still needed looking after. He was still a boy. They had to be careful.

He thought of Emily, his dear, departed wife of thirty-five years. She had been such a strong woman, righteous and vengeful.

She would have wanted this, would have wanted them to fight back. "You're the greatest," she told Carl each morning, coming up behind him as he stood before their full-length bedroom mirror, tying his tie. This was back when his hair was still dark brown, when he could get out of bed each morning without excruciating pain in his knees and hips. She'd wrap her tiny arms around his waist, so small her hands couldn't come together, and nuzzle her face against his back. "Go out there and take what's yours."

He curled his huge hands into fists. He'd crush the Underhill boy's skull if that's what it came to. He'd press his thumbs into his eyes and split his skull in two.

It was time. He was ready. They had to do it now.

"We keep it simple," Carl said. "Things go tits up when they get complicated. We walk right up there and knock on their front door. We force our way inside and we find the boy. Then we make him talk. They can't stop the three of us—not without a man in the house."

"And if they don't answer the door?" Hunter asked.

Carl tossed Frank a gold-plated Zippo. "Then we smoke 'em out."

He reached past Frank, grabbed the .38 from the glovebox, and slid it into the waistband of his jeans. He would do all the talking. He'd been a cop. He knew how to talk to people. He pressed the stun gun into Hunter's hand—didn't trust him with the real thing. If you need to use this, make sure he's close. Point blank. Then he told Frank to grab the shotgun. At least his son knew how to use it. After all, he'd taught him.

He didn't bother telling Frank that the shells were packed with rock salt. He didn't think it would matter. He didn't think Frank would ever need to pull the trigger. It likely wouldn't come to that. They had the element of surprise on their side. They had the power of fear.

They got out of the truck, slamming the doors a little too loudly. Carl was drunk, but he didn't realize how drunk until he was on his feet. The ground swayed and lurched beneath him. He burped, tasted bile. He placed his hand on the truck's side, braced himself, and made his way to the cargo bed. Then he grabbed one of the gas cans, put it on the ground near the rear tires. Frank grabbed the other two and did the same. Hunter went to the tree line and pissed.

"Remember," Carl said, as Hunter stumbled back to the truck, zipping his fly, an unlit cigarette dangling from his lips, "We're just here to talk. We just want to know the truth, right?"

"That's right," Hunter said, nearly barking. "We make that fucker talk."

"Keep your goddamn voice down," Frank said. "What the fuck is wrong with you?"

Hunter looked stung.

"Enough. Let's go."

The night was loud out in the deep woods, thick with insect hum. The deeper the woods, the louder darkness chittered, and out here was as deep as it got. Cool moonlight coated the world with an icy, silver shine, the light a streaking blur in Carl's alcohol-soaked vision.

They climbed a low concrete staircase, steps cracked and pierced by weeds, and crept onto the wide, hissing lawn. The windows of the house were still dark. No sound of movement inside. Carl felt his courage start to flag. This was insane. What the fuck were they doing? The thought occurred to him, all too late, that perhaps Emily wouldn't approve of this at all, remembering how old she'd looked just before she died, how gray, how tired. Are you crazy? she'd say. Have you lost your mind? What good could possibly come of this?

He didn't get the chance to turn back, to call it off. Motion lights kicked on, flooding the yard, blindingly bright, seemingly from every direction. He tried to shield his eyes.

Hunter froze in place.

Frank ducked off into the shadows alongside the house. Carl reached around and pulled the .38 from his waistband.

That was when the dogs came running. Two of them. Shepherds. Not even so much as a single bark, no warning whatsoever. Both dogs came bolting out of the darkness, running full speed. Before Carl could register what he was up against, one of them leaped into the air and slammed into him with its full weight. Carl's sheer size let him absorb the hit, pivoting and stepping back to maintain his balance. The dog attached its jaw to Carl's left forearm, grinding its teeth through the sleeve of his flannel.

Hunter turned and ran. The other dog closed him in on him fast.

Carl had just enough time to brace himself—fighting off one dog with his left arm—and aim for the other one with the .38. He suddenly felt stone-cold sober, clear-headed. Time slowed. He held his breath, got a bead on the dog chasing Hunter, and squeezed the trigger. The gunshot cracked. He saw the Shephard's fur ripple as the bullet slapped its ribs, puffed out a plume of pink mist on the other side. The dog spun around and landed with a dry thud.

Carl was just about to take care of the one attached to his arm when he felt his head go numb, his body go light. He stumbled forward and saw his wife way down there in a black void, her arms wide open. She was young again. As beautiful as he remembered. "You found me," she said, catching him as he fell forward into her arms. All the pain in his body, all the pain of old age disappeared. It felt like coming home after the longest, hardest day. He wept in her arms. "All this time I worried you weren't going to find me." She held him tight and together they spun headlong into the warmth of unending blackness.

STEPHEN UNDERHILL

A single candle burned bright in the center of the darkened stone chamber. The cool air smelled of earth—mineral-rich, the dust of eons past—the ripe smell of rebirth.

Stephen and Lettie sat cross-legged on the cold floor, facing each other, hands on their knees, the candle between them. They had both taken truly heroic doses of LSD. Stephen reached into his pocket and felt the glass vial, which he'd brought with him in the event they needed to push even further.

Beyond the human—what did anything matter anymore? Names were meaningless. Nothing was everything. He felt his human face melt away.

Stripped of skin, he thought, and left only with the smiling contours of the skull, all people were the same. The self was an illusion, the projection of electrical impulses coursing through the brain, an evolutionary development meant to propagate a cognitive, social species—and nothing else.

Soon enough, a fiery wind would wash all this away. All the surfaces that made up reality. God was a streetcleaner. All things would be swept into the endless gutter between the stars.

He closed his eyes and breathed in the smell of the soil, of bodies buried long ago, the tiniest spaces filled with minerals.

The tentacles of his mind tangled with Lettie's, twisting and tightening. Together they walked the obsidian shine of the abyss, the edge of the black mirror. Together they channeled their energies. A single mind. A single vision. The love of family. Blood. Memory. Fire.

When they'd first arrived in the chamber, they found a carving in the wall. A + N closed within the shape of a heart. Stephen ran his fingers over the jagged lines and felt the power of the room course through his body like an electric charge. This was the source. It was like he received a message from out of time, an expression of pure grief, weaving the strands of a new reality, a binding of the past and the present.

Together, the twins opened their many eyes and focused on the power of their blood, their connection with the spirits of the house. They dwelled in the chamber of the house's heart, channeling raw emotion. They dreamed in their rooms on the upper floors, bathed in the wordless language of sleeping giants. The true gods. The old gods. And from this well of pure consciousness, realized in the amygdala, emerged the wretched, broken spirit, from one side of the mirror to the other. Right away, Stephen sensed this thing shared their blood. They were getting closer to whatever it was they were searching for.

But something was wrong. This person was in so much pain. She emerged from the prison of the void in unbearable agony. This wasn't what was supposed to happen. This wasn't the way things were supposed to be. He saw his sister's face, her features flickering in the candlelight—in the fire—her mouth open, eyes sunken in shadow. She looked so scared.

Was this real? Was this really happening?

A sudden, terrible knowledge filled his mind, so much emotion and pain frantically pushing out at the seams of his skull. He saw the nighttime sky sour, stippled starlight bending into frayed, brittle strands. He saw the swirling pool of consciousness uncurl like a snake, lengthen into a twisted black current, a river of the damned, the souls of the dead and the dying swept away in terror, pulled toward the open mouth of the babbling, blind idiot at the center of the universe. Nothing but a cancer. A swirling mass of darkness and disease.

There was a rush of sound and light, the familiar acceleration of the acid, his neural networks lit up with enough electricity to animate a corpse. Only this time he was taken higher and further and faster than ever. He tasted his melting face. He saw infinite connections between infinite worlds, mapped in an alien geometry. He saw a giant, glistening squid in the depths of outer space, opening and closing its world-encrusted mouth, its suction-cup arms uncurling, releasing silver clouds of cosmic dust, its ancient eyes blinded by time.

The flame of the candle in the center of the room erupted with the strength of a blowtorch, masking the sound of the restless spirit's howling screams. A chorus of wild dogs. The ripping of flesh. There, in the bright light, he saw that he'd been mistaken. Lettie wasn't scared, no—she was enthralled.

The horror of the skull was that it could not look away. It could not close its eyes, those darkened, gaping sockets. The darkness ate light. The darkness was always hungry. The skull was doomed to bear witness. All that nothingness. Endless nothingness. Nothing was everything. Death could not look away.

This was what Lettie had always wanted. She wanted to fill the world with her pain.

He saw that now. He saw her for who she was.

She was death. She was disease.

They were the same.

He sat helplessly still as the spirit thrashed and screeched and tore its way into the world, crawling on all fours, the wretched thing. It was a woman. He saw that clearly—this thing was feminine in form. Her back was broken and twisted, long black hair obscuring her face. Her legs bent all the wrong ways, too many joints and in all the wrong places. She climbed onto the wall like a lizard, hair hanging like a curtain, revealing her open, bloodied mouth. Her jaw unhinged and her screams gave way to choking gurgles. Her discolored body convulsed once, twice, and then vomited out a fully grown man, naked, slick with slime. He fell far to the floor, skin scorched black, crusted, burnt. He opened his eyes, white with terror. He made sounds with his mouth but they didn't make sense.

The man climbed to his feet, wrapped his weird arms around the woman, still thrashing on the wall, and pulled her down to the floor. Their bodies slapped hard against the stone. They melted into each other so the man was in her place on the ground, twisting their limbs into knots. Then he was on top of her again, gripping her throat with both hands, baring his teeth, leaning his weight into it.

The flame burned brighter, a deep red. The dogs howled—their voices finding the same note, ascending. Everything was spinning out of control. The walls of the room oozed blood, scorched oil, the smell of rot, decay.

That was when Stephen saw the mummified child, still attached to its umbilical cord, its tiny, naked body. The thought occurred to him that women who died while pregnant could still expel the fetus—coffin birth, they called it, an utterly absurd pairing of words. And in those two words was the entirety of existence. Born into death. From one void to the next, trapped forever within the bent world of the black mirror. Whoever this was, she had been pregnant when she died. And she had died down here in the dirt and the darkness beneath the house, buried away. Secreted away. She'd given birth to a poor, lonely creature who was already dead, who had never even taken its first breath. This was the black seed from which blossomed all the pain, the terrible thing at the center of it all.

The wrestling, murderous forms of these two wretched souls dissolved into ribbons of black smoke, spinning through the stone chamber. The woman's howling grew louder, louder still. And then the trails of black smoke snaked beneath the low archway and spiraled up the stone steps that led to the house, a fiery wind in their wake, a trail of drifting embers.

Stephen tore free from his connection with Lettie and followed after them. He had to know who they were. He had to know where they were going. He had to know why. Lettie called out to him to stop, to come back, but he no longer recognized her voice.

He climbed the steps and entered the narrow, winding passageways. His sister's voice followed him. She begged him not to leave her in the dark. "I'm afraid," she said, "help me, don't leave me."

The stone walls ground like giant teeth as the hallways shifted and changed. Stephen struggled to push forward. A single step could cross a mountain, while the next might send him reeling over a shadowy precipice.

Somehow he made it back to the basement, ascending the staircase to the kitchen. Only abstractly did he register the skin-blistering heat of the door handle. He felt no pain. Motionless smoke filled the kitchen, thick and gray and toxic.

He turned the corner and saw the front room of the house engulfed in jumping, yellow flames. There was a rush of sound, wind whipping, wood cracking. It seemed so perfectly natural. He'd always known it would come to this—the cleansing power of fire. He'd always known. He fell to his knees, seized by a coughing fit. His eyes itched. He lay flat on his stomach, struggling to breathe.

From the moment he was born, when he was first given his name, his fate had been sealed. He was an Underhill. That was the significance of names. They could never be shed. They could never be undone. A person could never be unnamed.

There was no escaping his blood. He saw that now. Blood was everything, coursed through everything. He was just a name among so many other names, a single cell in the life stream. God help him. He felt the heat of so much anger. Each flickering tongue bore a black, slit-like pupil. He returned the gaze of the million eyes and knew then that the curse was real. It had come for them all.

And then the blackened form of a man stood before him. He was faceless, his white teeth shining in the light of the flames. His aura was pitch black. He was the embodiment of evil. Stephen suddenly felt that nothing was more important than ridding the world of this evil. He rose to his feet, grabbed a long knife from the kitchen counter. He moved forward to join its blade with this foul thing—whatever it was—that stood before him.

FRANKLYN BOWLES

The moment the motion lights came on—as bright as a football field on a Friday night—Frank knew they were fucked. Then the dogs came out of nowhere. Two of them.

It all happened so fast, a matter of seconds. His old man's gun went off, deafeningly loud. Frank's ears rang, muffling the sound. He stepped into the light, blinded. Hunter yelled something in a panic. One of the dogs growled. Large Carl wrestled with it, turned his back to Frank. Then a second gunshot sounded from somewhere in the distance, thunder cracking the sky, and the back of Carl's skull opened up.

It looked like a cheap special effect in a horror movie. It looked fake, the way his dad's head flapped open, exposing the bluish-white curve of blood-streaked bone. A chunk of dripping gore blew out the front of his dad's face and slapped the grass. The old man stumbled forward, his legs weirdly stiff, and let off a second shot from his .38 that bit into the ground at his feet, dirt flying up in the air. Then he fell forward—the frightened dog skittering out of the way—and crumpled in a heap.

Frank couldn't help it, couldn't control himself. He screamed.

He'd just seen the inside of his dad's skull, for fuck's sake.

The dog immediately turned its sights on him, locked its eyes on Frank. It started running, crossed ten, twenty yards in no time at all. Frank remembered those nights out on the field, beneath the bright lights, the sound of the crowd, the crisp autumnal air filling his lungs. He remembered how it felt to sprint up the line, a cornerback quickly closing the gap. There was no time to react—not in moments like those. There was only instinct—the shotgun in his hands. He racked a shell and fired from the hip. The sound was like cannon fire. But the dog was too fast. It lurched and leaped into the air—head tilted, paws curled against its chest, jaw hanging open—and hit Frank square in the chest. They went down together. Frank flung the gun away and tried to get his arms around the dog. It shook its head from side to side. Then it went for Frank's throat once, snapped its jaws, and again, strands of foamy spit hanging from its yellow teeth. It reared back for a third attempt and Frank had just enough time to throw a fast hook, clipping it hard on the nose.

The dog let out a high-pitched whine and stumbled back. Frank got his arms around its neck—a surge of adrenaline flowing through his veins—and got his leg over the dog's back. He kept one leg bent, his weight on his knee, and got the fucker in a chokehold. He squeezed its throat in the crook of his elbow, using his arm as a vice, flexing his bicep. The dog thrashed, panicking, breath rasping. Frank put his weight into it until he felt the animal weaken.

The dog went limp. He let it slip from his arms.

Then he was on his feet. He nudged the dog with his boot to see if it was alive or dead, awake or asleep. It didn't react. Its eyes were still open. Its reddish tongue spilled limp from its mouth. It wasn't breathing. Jesus God.

The lights still blared. Frank scanned the yard, the sight of his dad lying face down not registering as reality. The trees swayed in the nighttime wind. He saw the ten-gauge gleaming in the grass and took a step in its direction just as another bullet drilled into the ground behind him. The sky echoed with the sound of gunfire, as if on a delay. Frank took off running toward the truck. Fuck the shotgun. He didn't need it anymore. He needed to get out of the light.

All those years in the weight room, all through high school and college, doing countless cleans and lunges, working the jammer, all those explosive workouts, counting out the tempo, making sure to breathe, all that effort paid off in just this one moment, allowing him to push through the alcohol, how old he'd become, how out of shape, to push through the pain and the fear and the fatigue and into the safety of the darkness.

He came upon the truck only seconds later, saw Hunter inside the cab, his terrified face pressed up against the glass. The sight of it filled Frank with rage. Here he was getting shot at while Hunter hid away like a goddamn coward. Some things never changed— fuck no.

"Get out." Frank slapped the window with an open palm. He wanted his voice to sound forceful, to convey urgency, but instead, he sounded scared, desperate.

The door popped open and Frank grabbed Hunter by the collar of his shirt. He pulled his brother-in-law out of the cab, shoved him against the side of the truck, got right in his face. "They fucking killed my dad. And you're just sitting in here?"

He pretended like he couldn't see the hurt and confusion in Hunter's eyes. He pretended like he didn't feel the same way, like he wasn't scared out of his mind.

"We're doing this," Frank said. "Come on."

Hunter nodded. "Okay, man." And then, "I'm sorry, you know. About your dad. I don't know what to say. I don't know what happened. I heard the shots. I thought we'd all just go home."

Frank let go of Hunter's shirt. There was no time for this. He was so fucking mad. He checked to make sure he still had the lighter in his pocket, felt the cold metal with his fingers. Then he grabbed one of the gas cans. Hunter grabbed another one and followed, swinging the hammer at his side.

"Stay in the shadows," Frank said over his shoulder, keeping his voice low. "Someone's got a gun. Up high." He pointed toward the house—an open window in the gabled tower, maybe—or up in the trees. Above the barn? Over there on the second floor where the shutters were open? There were a million fucking places. God only knew which one.

Just as they reached the wide stone steps, the motion lights timed out and the yard went dark again. Frank and Hunter both froze in place, waiting to see if something would happen. Blood pulsed in Frank's ears. He half expected his head to get blown off. Finally, he let out his breath.

"No more dogs?" Hunter said.

"I don't think so. I don't know."

They both just stood there, listening. Frank tried to remember where he'd thrown the shotgun. He couldn't see it anywhere. It was too dark to see anything. Christ, what a mess. Everything had happened so quickly. How many shots had there been from above?

Two? The one that got his dad, the other one that nearly got him. That meant there was probably only one shooter. Maybe. Each shot was isolated, clean. The gun sounded like a rifle—it certainly did enough damage. One shooter, bolt-action, those things would give them enough time to make it across the yard, get to the house, bust open a window. He convinced himself this was the truth because it had to be the truth.

It was like Hunter knew what he was thinking. "Let me go first. Soon as those lights turn on, you make a break for the house. Don't run in a straight line. You'll make it."

There was no arguing with Hunter when he got that look in his eyes. "You sure?"

"It's the least I can do, man. You gotta trust me. I owe it to you. I'm the reason we're here right now. And you've already been shot at once tonight. Even's even."

Frank nodded. Hunter held out his hand and Frank took it, gripped it hard.

The lights kicked on and Hunter was gone, staying low as he ran across the yard, the gas can slapping his thigh. Frank followed, made a dash for it, cradling the gas can against his chest with both hands. His mind once more back on the football field, the ball tucked tight against his body, blowing past the outstretched arm of the cornerback.

The field was wide open—no one between him and the endzone. His life had meaning in that moment. He knew what he had to do and nobody could stop him.

Frank made it to the house just as Hunter busted out the front window with the hammer. They both dumped the gas cans through the window. Hunter went in first. Frank sliced up his hand pretty bad and snagged his jacket on a bent nail as he climbed over and fell against the floor.

The inside of the house was cavernous, cold. The ceilings were higher than he would have expected. It smelled like soil and rotting wood. Frank got the cap off the gas can and threw great sloshes of it against anything he could find, anything that looked like it would burn, the hallway runner, the curtains, a pair of warped sliding doors, an old armchair. Hunter did the same, making his way into an adjoining room. They reached the foot of a large staircase near the front door, Frank still dousing everything with gasoline. Hunter was smashing shit with the hammer, busting the place up. Then the can was empty. Frank tossed it to the ground. He pulled the lighter from his jacket pocket, held it in front of his face, relished the metallic snap of its cover flipping open.

Hunter looked at him wildly. "Do it, man. Light it up."

All Frank could think about was the inside of his dad's skull. How was it possible that any grown man could say he'd seen the inside of his dad's skull?

He felt the lighter's notched metal wheel with his thumb. The smell of gasoline made him feel lightheaded. How in the world had it come to this?

And then suddenly an old woman—as slight and pale as a ghost—glided soundlessly down that big old staircase, wearing nothing but a bright white nightgown. Frank saw the massive rifle she held in her thin arms. He saw the look of wild fury in her eyes, the white lines of her bloodless lips. He knew who she was and he felt no fear staring into the gaping black hole at the end of the gun's barrel.

The old woman smirked as she lined up the sights. "This is for Lou."

But she didn't sense Hunter Holbrook looming behind her, hammer raised in the air.

Frank flicked the wheel on the lighter, sparked the flame, and tossed it to the floor.

MARGARET UNDERHILL

Most people, regular folks, they saw the full moon as a kind of cosmic culmination, a symbol of harvest, or spiritual fulfillment—the mother energy. They saw something meaningful in the harmonious alignment of the Earth, the Moon, and the Sun. They saw rhyme and reason, a greater purpose, or some grand design. Peg saw something different. To her, the full Moon was a cup brimming over. It was a heart aching with too much love, too much sorrow.

The phases of the moon waxed and waned as if on a wheel, always turning, alternating between two extremes: the new and the old, the full and the hollow. And at the center of this wheel, holding everything together, a vast and unknowable power. An all-seeing eye.

Magic was most potent on nights like these. Tails of smoke lingered longer. The tides swelled with black waters, rippling in the light. And people, regular folks, they did things they would normally never do, acting on impulses they hid even from themselves, as if rooted in their darkest desires. That was what people didn't get about the full moon, the way the light masked the dark, seeping up from beneath.

Peg stood over the kitchen sink, filled a mason jar with water, and took a sip. Something—a bad dream perhaps, or maybe a premonition—had compelled her out of bed. The tiled floor was cold beneath her bare feet. The house was quiet and dark; the air was stuffy. She forced open the window above the sink and breathed in the sweet smell of trees, tried to read the air's personality. The spirits had gone silent in anticipation, but of what?

The answer arrived as a diesel pickup wound its way up the long drive, the yellow beams of its headlights sweeping over the yard. That was when she knew—knew in her heart—nothing would ever be the same, not after tonight.

Carlton Bowles emerged from the truck, a giant man wearing dusty jeans, leather boots, and a flannel shirt. The others followed, the boy's father and uncle, both of them big, ungainly. All three were noticeably drunk, arguing loudly. They may have possessed strength, but their senses were dulled.

Peg watched with increasing unease as they took gas cans out of the truck and placed them on the ground. They had come to destroy everything her family had built, everything House Underhill stood for. But they had underestimated her if they thought she'd let them do it without a fight.

She moved quickly, went to the den and swung the wheel on the gun safe, grabbed the biggest rifle she had, the one that would inflict the most damage, the .375 H&H Magnum. The thing weighed a lot for her tired old arms, but still, she summoned the strength. She knew the gun well, knew she'd be able to handle its kick.

Kate and Minnie were alert in their kennel out back, waiting for their commands. "Quiet." She kept her voice firm. They looked at her with their big black eyes, purely obedient. They were good dogs, two of the best she'd ever owned, but they were also the protectors of her legacy. They had jobs to do. She slipped both dogs a treat before repeating the command, unlatching the kennel gate.

The dogs flanked her as she crept around the side of the house—and just in time. The motion sensor lights popped on. The world went bright, casting long shadows.

Peg issued the dogs' attack command. They took off in the direction of the men. She followed after them, turning the corner, making sure to stay out of sight. There was a tussle with the old man. Holbrook took off running. Peg couldn't pinpoint Frank. The dogs would take care of the other two. She needed to incapacitate Frank. He was the most dangerous. Then Carl let off a shot from a pistol she hadn't seen and Peg saw Minnie spin to the ground. Filled with sudden, blinding rage, Peg pressed the rifle stock to her shoulder, tilted her head, got the back of the old man's head in her sights, and squeezed the trigger.

The sound of the shot phased into the distance as Carlton dropped out of sight, let off a wild shot with his pistol—no telling where it might have gone. Then Peg retreated. She needed to find higher ground. She needed to find the twins. Surely they heard the gunshots. Surely they were frightened, confused. She whistled for Kate but the dog didn't return. By the time Peg reached the back door, she heard the blast of a shotgun, and her blood ran cold.

She locked the door behind her and made her way upstairs, calling for the twins. She tried to slow her breathing, steady her hands. She'd just killed a man, but damned if he hadn't had it coming. Peg opened the door to Stephen's room. His bed was empty. She crossed the hall. Lettie wasn't in her room either, her snake's terrarium the only light.

Where the hell were they? Had they snuck out?

The big window overlooking the front yard was open. It was one of Lettie's favorite spots. Peg crossed the room and sat on the cushioned bench with her back against the wall, breathing. She surveyed the grounds below. Everything was still lit up, motion sensors still going. There he was, Frank, stumbling into view. Peg quickly lined up the shot, not sure if she'd get another chance, but she was too eager. She was too worried about the twins. Frank ducked out of the way just before she squeezed the trigger. The bullet went wide, ripped a fat divot in the dirt.

Peg's rage returned. She'd given up her position for nothing. She left the open window, returned to the hallway, calling out once more for Lettie and Stephen, a little more frantic this time, a little less sure they were merely hiding.

Then she heard something that made her freeze in place, something she hadn't heard in years. She stood still, listened to the sounds of the house. The old joints cracked. The rafters moaned. And underneath those familiar sounds, from far below the ground, Peg heard those strange sounds that haunted her childhood. She heard the tortured howls of the trapped souls in the caves, heard something long buried claw its way to the surface.

Peg was overcome with resignation, the black that wormed its way up from beneath the light. Everything she'd done to protect her family, to preserve their way of life, to keep the past in the past, it was all coming undone from within. She slid to the ground with her back against the wall, the rifle crossed over her thighs.

It was as if an invisible hand gripped her body, pressed her arms tight against her ribs. She was filled with an entire lifetime of dread.

She felt her breathing slow, her vision dim. How easy it would have been to give herself over to the fear, to let it overtake her.

The sound of breaking glass came from somewhere downstairs. They were inside the house. No, she couldn't let them win. They'd already taken so much from her. She'd already lost so much. The memory of Lucretia flashed through Peg's mind, the car carrying her daughter and Saint Pete engulfed in flame, a fireball twisting red into the nighttime sky. She had to do this for Lou.

Her old bones screamed as she climbed to her feet, the weight of the rifle seemingly more than she could bear. They were downstairs, tearing the place apart, smashing things. She made her way down the long staircase. The smell of gasoline was unmistakable.

She reached the bottom of the staircase. Frank Bowles held a lighter, his thumb on the wheel.

Frank's eyes met hers as she raised the gun. He knew she was going to kill him and he didn't care. He was ready to die. So be it. These people would never stop coming for her and her family.

"This is for Lou."

Frank turned the wheel on the lighter and the flame bloomed a bright yellow. Peg's finger curled around the trigger. And before he'd even let the lighter go, before he'd even tossed it to the gasoline-soaked runner at the foot of the stairs, she let off a shot that punched a hole through his chest. The bullet took an entire panel out of the door behind him.

Frank was thrown back just as the lighter thumped against the floor. Fire raced throughout the room, blue at first, roaring and crackling as it turned yellow, then orange, everything going up in an instant. The heat was skin blistering, inescapable. Before Peg could even begin to panic, before she could even chamber another bullet, something clubbed her hard on the back of the head. She stumbled forward, the gun clattering to the floor, and crashed against the banister with her shoulder.

One of her eyeballs was loose. She felt it pinched, pulsing with pain. She'd bit her tongue, blood in her mouth. Her right foot wouldn't stop twitching, tapping rapidly against the floor.

A black wind swooped through the room. From the fire? No, this was something else entirely. It was unnatural, the way it whipped itself into wide circles. It blew into the room and swept away the fire. It swept everything away like it was nothing. The stillness in its place offered a glimpse of a moment frozen in time, somehow there but not there. Peg saw a vision of the past, a scene she did not recognize, the faces of people she did not know. She saw an old, unrecognizable house on the land where House Underhill now stood. She saw a fire raging beneath the full moon, not unlike this one. All of these things had always been here. They had always been lurking, waiting to be recalled, to be seen anew.

The flames in her vision merged with the flames before her now. They returned with renewed strength, engulfing her. She felt her skin cracking, splitting open.

Her screams were inhuman, even to her, as if pulled through time, merging with the memories of her forebears. It was the sound of a thousand wronged women all crying out in shared agony. There was the one in the early days of man walking the earth, a woman whose naked body was abandoned by her tribe, left to dry out beneath the sun on a bed of razor-sharp igneous stone, and then another in the middle ages, drawn and quartered, each of her limbs roped to black stallions. There were those burned at the stake by the Holy Roman Empire and those tried and hanged in

Salem, surrounded by so many ugly, prideful faces. And there was the one here in Stone River, a sweet girl who never knew her place in the world, trapped alone in the dark of the mines, and forgotten by everyone who had loved her.

How Peg's heart ached for her, this girl whose name she did not know, and for all who came before her, all of them utterly destroyed, their bones ground to dust, their ashes scattered in the wind. She let go of her rage and gave it to them, where perhaps it would prove more useful, restore balance once and for all. She let the flames take her and within their loving caresses, she found the fortitude to rise to her feet, channeled the power she needed to complete one last action, the final turn of the wheel.

HUNTER HOLBROOK

Hunter sat in the back seat of the truck's cab, trying to see what was going on. He had no idea what was happening. His hands shook. He couldn't catch his breath. The last thing he remembered was seeing the dogs, getting chased by one of them, then hearing the first gunshot. He'd nearly shit himself, it was so loud.

He'd tried to tell Frank and Carl this was a bad idea, that they shouldn't be doing this, that they shouldn't be here. And now he was going to wind up back in prison. No. He'd kill himself before that happened. The moment he saw flashing lights, he'd kill himself. He turned the stun gun over in his hands and sighed. They hadn't even given him a real gun.

He remembered the night before Orn disappeared. He hadn't been able to sleep, lying awake on the couch in Frank and Court's living room, torturing himself with thoughts of Sweet Lou, recalling the shape of her teeth when she smiled, her single dimple. At some point, maybe around two or three in the morning, he got up and went out on the front porch to smoke a cigarette. Minutes later, Orn emerged from the dark and stepped into the porchlight. He was drunk, slurring his speech, stumbling around. His eyes were all pupils. His arm was wrapped in a ripped T-shirt, crusted with dried blood. Hunter had a hundred questions. Are you okay? What happened to you? Where have you been? Where's your Jeep? But Orn just kept raving. Nothing he said made any sense. He talked about invisible demons, about being followed by a giant floating eyeball, about how he'd been born with bad blood.

Hunter was worried they might wake up Court. She would have lost her mind if she saw Orn like that. She would have blamed Hunter for setting a bad example, for being such a fuck-up. So he grabbed the keys to Frank's Cadillac and drove Orn around for an hour or so, just to get him away from the house. Maybe they could talk it out. Maybe Orn just needed to come down. But he just kept saying the same things over and over again. Everything he said—the way he said it, with such resignation in his voice, such fear—made Hunter feel crazier and crazier.

Then there was a strange moment of clarity. Orn emerged from the swirl of madness, peeked out from behind the confusion. The car rolled to a stop at a red light. Hunter looked at his nephew in the dim light from the dash and saw nothing more than a scared little boy.

"It's a curse," Orn said. "None of us can escape it."

Hunter felt his heart drop. He saw himself getting behind the wheel of his car the night Sweet Lou died, the night he'd killed her. He realized now, all these years later, that he'd also killed their unborn child. Of course, it was theirs. He'd known the moment Carl told him she'd been pregnant. He'd known because he'd felt the loss, somehow he'd always known. Of all the people in the world, he'd crashed into her, as if guided by an invisible hand.

"You know what I mean," Orn said. "I can see it in your eyes. You know."

Orn flung open the door, jumped out of the car, and ran. The darkness of the woods opened up and swallowed him whole. Hunter let him go. He was too tired and too freaked out to go after him. He was too worried about leaving Frank's car. It was the last time he saw his nephew alive.

He hadn't told anyone about that night. Court was already so mad. She'd already threatened to kick him out. If she kicked him out, he'd have nowhere to go. No one wanted him around. He knew that if he ever got kicked out he'd wind up back in prison. Hell, he really did think Orn would be home in the morning.

There was movement outside the truck. Hunter pressed his face against the glass and nearly screamed when he saw Frank peering back at him. Frank slapped the glass with his hand. Hunter unlocked the door and suddenly Frank's hands were around the collar of his shirt.

At first, Hunter thought Frank was going to strangle him. Then he thought he was going to hit him. But Frank wasn't angry, not exactly. He was something else. He was scared. He might have even been in shock. He said that Carl was dead. Hunter didn't know what to say. He never fucking knew what to say. So he just said the first thing that came to mind, something dumb.

All of this had gone too far. That's what Orn had been trying to tell him. Frank and Hunter each grabbed a gas can. Hunter grabbed the hammer. Together they set off toward the house.

When they reached the lawn and the bright lights, Hunter decided he should be the one to go first. He didn't care if there was someone out there with a gun. All he had to do was remember what life had been like in prison. He had nothing to lose. He didn't hesitate. He ran. And when he got to the house he couldn't believe he was still alive. For the first time in a long time, it felt so good to be alive. He bashed out the window with the hammer, cleared away the shards of glass.

Once they were inside, all of Hunter's fear, all of his regrets, his guilt—it all came flooding back.

The gas cans were empty. Hunter dropped the empty can to the floor. Frank did the same. He stood in the archway across the foyer, pulled the lighter out of his pocket, the clean sound of the metal cap snapping open. Hunter took a step back into the kitchen, the big staircase between them.

And that was when the old woman came down the stairs, carrying that big-ass rifle. Hunter raised the hammer up over his head just as Frank turned the wheel on the lighter, just as he dropped it onto the rug, just as the old woman pulled the trigger. The whole room shook from the sound. The fire was everywhere, spreading fast, thick with smoke. Before Frank's body even hit the ground, Hunter brought down the hammer on the back of the old woman's head, felt its impact scrape along the curve of her skull. A dark gash bloomed beneath her ghostly white hair, and the old woman stumbled forward into the flames. She cried out, dropped the heavy rifle, and slammed into the banister of the staircase. Her foot was thumping against the floor like she was having some kind of seizure.

Hunter watched as her nightgown caught fire, turned black, and disintegrated, as her silver hair lit up bright orange and burned away to nothing, as her skin blistered and popped. She went up so fast—faster than he would have thought possible. He raised his forearm over his eyes to block the heat, already blinded from the smoke, the intensity of the flames, and took a step back into the kitchen.

He turned just in time to see Stephen Underhill come at him with a butcher knife, slashing away like a maniac in a horror film. He got the stun gun free and fired off the plugs, which hit Stephen in the neck, generating a couple of useless orange sparks, electricity crackling. Stephen didn't even slow down. He brought down the knife and Hunter felt it bite into his shoulder, then his chest. The cool blade dragged down along his bicep before he got a hold of the kid's arm. He had Stephen by the wrist, his arm cocked back, the knife's wavering blade gleaming in the light of the flames.

Hunter felt no fear. If anything, he was amazed by how much Stephen looked like Orn that night on the front porch. They shared the same madness—galaxy deep—it was in their eyes. And even though Hunter had a hundred pounds on this kid, even though he could have easily snapped back his wrist, he found himself unable to do so. Maybe it was a trick of the light, the sparks flying from the plugs in the kid's neck, all that smoke from the fire clouding his mind, or maybe it was the shadows cast by the flames, but Hunter could have sworn he was wrestling his nephew.

Stephen kicked Hunter in the shin, then the kneecap. Hunter felt something come loose. He dropped to his other knee, wrenched his back, still holding onto the kid's wrist. And then, just as Hunter opened his mouth to scream, Stephen reached around with his free hand and poured some kind of liquid down Hunter's throat, enough of it to cause him to gag. He turned to the side and spit it out across the floor.

Hunter had taken enough hits of acid in his life to know when he'd been dosed. But even then, nothing could have prepared him for this, for how quickly this stuff took control of his mind, for how total and all-consuming the fear and panic were that came over him.

And at that moment he knew what Orn had been talking about. He understood about the invisible demons, the floating eyeball. There was all this invisible stuff all around them. Living nightmares that couldn't be seen by the naked eye. He felt himself raised from this world by skinless gargoyles, their long-fingered hands nothing but muscle and bone, batting their wings. They stretched his skin over the surface of the Moon. He felt the billions of eyeballs of the universe—the crooked black sky littered with stars—crawling over him, inside of him. He had been exposed, his soul laid bare for all to see.

And there was Orn, striding across the eternal plane, the curve of the black mirror between two worlds. As he came close, Hunter saw the orange streaks of meteor showers reflected in Orn's pupils, as large as planets. Pure black stones. Cosmic eggs. He saw smoke twisting into the sky, billowing off the wreckage of a flaming car. And he heard the endless laughter of Sweet Lou echoing in the depths of outer space.

He wanted so badly to believe that everything wasn't his fault because deep down inside he knew that it was. He woke the curse from its slumber. He had given life to a child that bore the blood of both families, the shadow of the child that came before, and he too had taken it away.

What gave him the right to do such a thing?

The old woman came to him—Margaret—she came to him engulfed in flames. Her skin had burned away. Her charred skull was visible within the yellow corona of pure, cleansing light. Her eyes ungazing, jaw hinged open in an eternal smile.

He held out his arms to welcome her, believing that if he died with her there, in this house, he would end the curse forever. She threw her arms around him and the two of them burned together. Together they found fullness. They became the light. Their bloodlines fused. Hunter held onto these thoughts as tightly as he could. He could hear Sweet Lou's sobs of joy, her cries of relief.

He saw the shape of her smile, swimming in an ocean of sunlight.

He finally knew what it was to feel forgiveness.

A HOTEL ROOM BY THE HIGHWAY

Lettie was adrift inside a small black room, recalling the feeling of being trapped, shaking with fear among the centipedes and the pill bugs, overlooked during all that fiery chaos. She reached out to touch the wall and felt it give way to endless space.

She maintained steady eye contact with Barbara as she talked about how the cops found her the next day hiding in the stone cellar, miraculously unscathed, curled in a ball. She talked about how they wrapped her in a blanket and led her out of the darkness and into the daylight, helped her climb over a half-charred roofbeam, and scramble up a pile of steaming rubble. Coming up and out of the dark, the world never felt so vast, so emptied out and gray. Everything radiated intense, fusty heat. Feathers of ash drifted slowly through the air. The smell of it—so many memories, the essence of things that no longer existed, so much bone dust— gave her an instant, grinding headache.

A plain-clothes cop with a silver mustache handed her a stuffed bear. For comfort, he said. She sat on a gurney in the back of an ambulance, holding the bear. Someone else strapped an oxygen mask over her face, told her to breathe deep. They covered her with a scratchy blanket. Then they shut the doors. She heard the occasional scramble of radio static, loopy, in a daze. It was almost as if she wasn't there at all, as if no one could see her.

Ever since then, she told Barbara, she couldn't remember not feeling that way—separate from everyone else, shut away behind closed doors. She couldn't remember ever belonging anywhere, feeling at home. All of that had been ripped away from her.

Nearly all of House Underhill had burned away during the long night, the only home Lettie had ever known. What remained, amazingly, was a blackened, skeletal structure that was entirely unfamiliar, the ancient wooden frame of a much older, smaller house. Some of the original brickwork and wall studs had survived, flame scarred, ashen. Lettie eventually recognized the ruins within the ruins as their living room, the fireplace around which they celebrated so many Christmas mornings still standing, perfectly intact.

"What were you and your brother doing in the basement?" Barbara said, the suddenness of her question pulling Lettie out of her memories and bringing her back to the present, back beneath the bright lights, the cameras. "Why were you down there at that hour?"

Lettie had anticipated this. She stuck to the version of events she'd given at the trial. Everything had to be consistent. She had to answer Barbara's questions in a way that didn't lead to more questions. That's what this was all about: providing closure.

"Stephen wanted to show me something he'd found. I told you how he'd been researching our family history, going to the library and reading old newspapers, the kinds of things kids did in movies. Well, that summer we discovered that our basement was connected to the old mines, and Stephen had reason to believe that someone had been trapped down there a long time ago. Call it intuition. Someone we were related to, who'd never been found. He didn't think it was right that she should be forgotten. He wanted her spirit to find rest. We didn't know what we were looking for. We just wanted to explore. So we dug up some old maps, grabbed some flashlights, and went down there."

"In the middle of the night?"

"It was against our grandmother's rules to go into the tunnels. She said they were dangerous. She was right, of course. It wasn't safe. Some of the passages were flooded. The old support beams had rotted. We grew up hearing horror stories about blackdamp." Lettie paused. "But we were teenagers. We didn't care. So we went down there at night when she was asleep."

"Did you find what you were looking for?"

Lettie remembered Stephen leading her to the stone chamber, the beams of their flashlights sweeping through the mine's narrow tunnels, everything crawling with dust and cobwebs. It was so claustrophobic, so dark. She remembered her sense of space expanding as they entered the chamber, the mineral-rich smell of its dirt floor, the sensation of the cool air filling her lungs. She remembered the way the room felt charged with a mysterious power, the way it called to her.

Right away she realized it was a special place. She longed to connect with it, learn its secrets. Stephen shined his flashlight at the carving in the wall. Lettie ran her fingers over the small, sharp etchings. A + N within the shape of a heart.

Stephen clicked off the flashlight, struck a match—the hiss and flare of the flame bathing the chamber in a wavering orange glow—

and lit the candle he'd placed on the floor. He instructed Lettie to sit down. Then she heard the familiar, delicate tinkling sound of the glass eye dropper being removed from its vial, followed by her brother's voice, from somewhere beyond the candlelight. "Reveal to me your eye."

"We didn't find anything," Lettie said. "There was nothing down there but water and rats. It didn't take long for us to get lost. I still have nightmares about it. We got turned around in the tunnels and I got scared. At some point, I don't remember when, we heard gunshots up above. That was just about the time we found our way back to the basement. Stephen went upstairs to investigate. He told me to stay behind because I was so scared." And then, for good measure, "I hid in the root cellar. Probably the safest room in the entire house."

Barbara seemed to consider this for a moment. Lettie saw the way the lines in Barbara's face, barely detectable beneath all that heavy makeup, changed when she decided on a question. "What do you believe happened to your brother?"

"Stephen died in the fire."

"But his remains were never recovered."

"The house was completely consumed by the fire. That was the term they used. Even my pet snake died, so far as I know."

Barbara was undeterred. "Your grandmother, Franklyn Bowles, Hunter Holbrook—all three were identified by their remains. Your brother was not among them. What do you make of that?"

Lettie stayed cool. "If I were to believe that Stephen is still alive, I would also have to accept that in the years since the fire he's never once tried to contact me." She softened her eyes. "I'm sorry, but I can't bring myself to do that. The idea that Stephen is out there somewhere and that he hasn't tried to talk to me is worse than the thought of him being dead." She allowed her voice to tremble. "Does that make sense?"

That morning years ago, lying on the gurney in the back of the ambulance, holding that stupid stuffed bear, they closed the doors on her and drove her to the hospital. The basement kept her safe during the fire, but there was still the risk of smoke inhalation, or so they said. Really they wanted to keep watch over her, monitor her.

Lettie gradually learned what had happened from the cops who came to visit her. They spent hours asking her questions. Sometimes they asked her the same question twice back to back, other times they waited, tried to be sneaky about it. It didn't take her long to put the pieces together. She learned that Scud first called the police when his dad didn't come home that night, that her grandmother was dead, that her brother was missing, presumed dead.

"Can we talk about what happened next?" Barbara said. "That night at the hospital?"

Lettie took a deep breath. "Yes. I'm ready."

She didn't wait for Barbara to ask a question. She just started talking. She needed this part to sound unrehearsed.

She told the story the only way she could. Parts of it she remembered. Other parts she knew only from the news reports, from what she'd been told. Those parts, the ones she did not remember, were seemingly stronger than her memories, more real somehow.

Lettie couldn't sleep that night in the hospital, not with all those nurses checking in on her, changing this or that, not with all the noise from those machines, the various alarms and buzzers that screamed at all hours. And so she lay in her bed, staring at the ceiling, turning over the events of the past few days in her mind, the grief of losing her grandmother, the rage that coursed through her veins, feelings stronger than any sedative they might have given her.

And it was in that state, overtired and confused and heartbroken, that Lettie heard two of the nurses talking at their station. They spoke loudly, making no effort to hide their voices. She heard them talk about how Courtney Bowles was being restrained and sedated after a suicide attempt, that she had threatened to kill herself again after she learned about the death of her husband. And then—shockingly—she heard them say that Court was in a room just down the hall.

Lettie remembered that day in the grocery store, when Court had drawn back her arm and slapped her across the mouth. She remembered the sting of it, the embarrassment, the sheer anger that flooded her senses, the feeling of hatred boiling over.

Maybe it was the drugs they'd given her, maybe it was her exhaustion, but it was almost as if she watched herself from outside herself, helpless to control her actions. She waited for the nurses to finish their conversation, to do their rounds, and then she patiently unhooked herself from all the wires, got out of bed, and went down the hall. Nobody stopped her. Nobody seemed to notice her at all.

She soon found Courtney Bowles's room and ducked inside, quietly shutting the door behind her. It was dark, the shades drawn tight. The lights on the machines glowed. Lettie stood over Court as she slept. She saw how Court's hands were fastened to the bedrails with straps. She listened to Court's rhythmic breathing. Then she took a pillow from behind Court's head and put it over her face. One of the machines near the bed started beeping faster. The tendons in Court's arms tightened. She thrashed against her restraints, her moaning muffled by the pillow. Lettie summoned every ounce of strength she had. The machine beeped faster, faster—each moment an eternity—and then flatlined.

The door to the room swung open and the silhouette of a nurse filled the doorway, surrounded by light. "My God, what have you done?"

Lettie remembered releasing the pillow, turning to the nurse, tears streaming down her face.

The light from the hallway was replaced by the box lights of the hotel room. The shocked look on the nurse's face replaced by Barbara's sympathetic expression. The high-pitched squeal of the flatline replaced by the silence of a room full of people collectively holding their breath.

"My lawyer argued that I was under the influence of drugs. He said that I was confused and that I shouldn't have been held responsible for my actions. I thought Mrs. Bowles was going to kill me in my sleep. She blamed me for her son's death. Her whole family did. They attacked us in our home. She was bound to discover I was in the same hospital as her, just like I had. That's what my lawyer argued during the trial."

Barbara said nothing. She knew when to simply listen.

"But that wasn't the truth. I never should have taken my lawyer's advice. Nobody believed that I was in any danger—not after what happened. Courtney Bowles was a broken woman. She'd lost nearly everything. Honestly? I felt bad for her. I believed that killing her was the right thing to do. It's what she wanted. She wanted to die, right? I thought killing her was the only way to end the curse. It was a win-win."

Barbara seemed to consider what this meant for the story, what it meant for the interview. Her eyes were ravenous. "And what do you believe now? Do you think you ended it?"

There was a moment, lying on the gurney in the back of the ambulance, when Lettie first felt herself adrift in the black room. It was a room of unknown dimensions, with walls that occasionally felt as close and cramped as a casket. Other times it felt as vast as the universe itself. She had never escaped its walls. Always she was reminded of their presence. Always she felt them looming.

And as she was pulled away from the smoking remnants of House Underhill, from everything she'd known, she let the black room surround her. She didn't even notice when she plucked the black plastic eyes from the stuffed bear and let them clatter against the ambulance floor.

"No. There was still so much I didn't understand."

"Such as?"

"Well, for one, it's not really my story. It was never about me or Orn, or Hunter Holbrook and my mom." This was the part where she would free herself once and for all. "When I was in prison, I did a lot of reading. I read pretty much everything that was published about me and my family, about the massacre, my trial, and the aftermath. All these things are just echoes in time. I found a photo of House Underhill after it burned down that showed the chimney that used to be in our living room. It was still standing. And if you look closely at the brickwork it's attached to—the same walls that were covered up and built over in the house I lived in—you'll see that children had carved their initials into the brick. Next to their initials, they carved notches to show how much they'd grown each year." Lettie paused. "There were three of them—three kids. And one of them was a girl named Agatha. Agatha Underhill. And there, next to her initials, the number three and a notch some two and a half feet tall. Then ages, five, eight, ten, fourteen—the notch always getting taller. And then nothing."

Lettie recalled the cries of the black-haired women in the stone chamber, the restless spirit with the bloodied mouth, the woman who emerged from the void, who had turned to smoke, a force of pure rage and revenge. The sound of those cries would haunt her until her dying day.

"Agatha Underhill had always been there. Inside the house. She made her mark, only to be secreted away within its walls, her bones buried in the dirt of the tunnels. It's with her that the curse began. All those years, all that fighting between the two families, the murders and the crimes, it was always because of her. It's her story that needs to be told."

AGATHA UNDERHILL, THE SUMMER OF 1833

She was the kind of young woman who always put the needs of others before her own. She spent Sunday mornings shepherding the little ones at the newly constructed Wesleyan Missionary, her evenings setting the supper table, repeating her father's prayers as she held tight the hot-blooded hands of her two younger brothers. And when night fell, she sat by their bedsides and recited the familiar lines of fairy tales and fables, her round, radiant face glowing gold in the lamplight.

After church, Agatha ran errands for her mother. She was seventeen then, old enough to be out on her own. Or so she'd argued, eventually wearing down her father's reluctance, eliminating his stubbornness through sheer force of will.

She loved being among the bustle of everyday life, the horse-drawn carriages that kicked up clouds of dust, the overheard bits of conversation. She loved the weight of coins in her dress pockets. Sometimes she lingered near the public auction and watched folks bid on chickens and old farm tools. Other times she was content to watch children jump rope or play games of Annie Over.

One such day—a beautiful, sunny afternoon—Agatha left the apothecary having purchased cod liver oil and inhaling hemlock for her grandmother's consumption. The world was in full bloom, the air sweet as flowers. She passed through the whitewashed wood-frame houses clustered near the mouth of the river, all recently constructed by her father's company to shelter the miners. Thin-faced men and women watched as Agatha paraded by in her Sunday best, her polished shoes, her carefully braided hair, perfectly oblivious to their cold glares, the stubborn stains of coal dust.

Back then, the settlement was known as Copper Creek, though there was no copper to be found. Some said it was named as such for the brown-tinted waters that fed into the Mississippi. Others said the name was a clever ruse to lure the downtrodden and the desperate. Either way, it attracted all walks of life. There were honest folks looking for work, and there were those who, for whatever reason, sought new beginnings. All were welcome, so far as Agatha was concerned. That's what she'd learned in church. Every soul had a place in the world. That's what she believed in her heart. All need to be saved. All may be saved to the uttermost.

A gray mist rose from the narrow-banked river, its tendrils ghostly silent. And there, on the other side, Agatha saw the two magnificent red-brick chimneys of House Underhill, perched high upon its hill, looking out over the town below, a sight that filled her heart with happiness and gratitude.

She was blessed, she thought, approaching the house. Life was good and God was great.

Agatha entered the kitchen through the back door and found her mother preparing supper, something she took great pride in managing on her own. An iron pot boiled on the stove in the center of the room and the sharp smell of burning hickory filled the air. "Did you get your grandmother's medicine?" Agatha's mother said, beautiful as ever in her white kitchen dress, sweat-damp curls framing her small, flushed face. "Go on then. You know where to find her."

Her brothers, young and reckless, nearly careened into her as she entered the living room. She smiled as she heard them thump through the kitchen, her mother yelling after them.

Agatha made her way down the long cramped hall and past her father's study. There he sat behind his desk, wearing his spectacles and a buttoned pullover shirt. He appeared to be reviewing documents spread over his desktop, deep in concentration, the room thick with tobacco smoke. The poor man was a slave to his work, even on the Lord's day.

She opened the front door and stepped onto the porch. The wide lawn stretched as far as she could see, endless as an ocean. Winds pressed over the green grass, darkening slightly in the shifting sunlight. Her grandmother sat still in her rocking chair, legs covered with a heavy wool blanket and shoulders wrapped in a shawl.

Agatha's grandmother was a strikingly beautiful woman. She wore her silver hair long, parted down the middle and tied back with a gorgeous green ribbon. Her features had somehow sharpened with age.

Agatha removed the blood-spattered handkerchief from the old woman's hand, where it was wrapped tightly around two slender fingers. For a moment, she marveled at how much her grandmother's skin felt like paper, bloodless and thin. Then she retrieved the bottle of cod liver oil, removed the stopper, and carefully filled the spoon with the syrupy, yellow liquid. Her grandmother took the medicine without fuss.

The blood-orange sun fattened in the sky, lulled low in the pale fade of evening. Wrapped in the warmth of that moment, Agatha felt a deep sense of calm come over her—of peacefulness and belonging—interrupted only by her mother's call that supper was ready.

These were the best days of her life. She knew that even then.

Later that night, Agatha got out of bed. She undid the latch on her window and pushed open its hinged casement, the heavy panes of hand-blown glass briefly catching the moonlight as they swung outward. A moment later she saw the flame of a matchstick in the distance.

The house was quiet, bathed in cold silver. Its darkened, empty spaces ached in the silence, corners crawling with shadow. Agatha snuck downstairs, out the front door, and crossed the yard. The grass was cool beneath her bare feet. When she drew close, Nathaniel Bowles emerged from the shadows. He wore a dark coat, light trousers, and leather boots. His hair was a mess of curls. She went to him without hesitation and he held her tightly, kissed the top of her head. His outpouring of affections were lost to the thrum of her heartbeat, the deafening pulse of blood in her ears.

It was like a dream—the night's deep mystery, the play of light, the smell of his perfume. How she relished the chill in the air and the warmth of his embrace. But then his words took shape in her mind, becoming unpleasantly real, thrusting her into the waking world. "What did you say?" She tilted her head, looking up into his shadow-pooled face.

"I said run away with me. We shall leave tonight."

She stepped away from him, and he let her go, sensing that something was wrong.

"You know I can't do that. I could never leave my family."

"Agatha, please. It's the only way for us to be together. The men in town are starting to talk. They're meeting in one of the taverns at night. They say your father—"

She knew what they said. She'd heard it all—lies, all of it the most egregious lies. Her father was a magnanimous man. He'd opened the mines only five years ago and already hundreds of men were in his employ. Those men were happy. They were well looked after. It wasn't until Nathaniel's father, Ephraim, started spreading such hateful rumors that things had spoiled. He stood there in the town square, telling anyone who would listen that Underhill's mines were unsafe, that pay was too low by half. Ever since then, people said that Agatha's father hired men whose reputations could not be vouched for. They said he was a tyrant. Someday soon, they said, the workers would rise up and take what was theirs.

No, she did not need to hear these things once more. She could not bear it. And so she interjected, saying precisely why she bid his presence that night. "My love, I'm with child."

A long, drawn-out silence followed. The din of crickets filled the lull. Agatha searched the shadows. She tried to detect the look on Nathaniel's face, and nearly jumped out of her skin when he lit yet another matchstick, the hiss of the flame as ferocious as a copperhead. The sharp lines of his teeth were briefly etched in the dark, blood-red, as he touched the dancing flame to the tip of a hand-rolled cigarette.

There was a hint of distrust in his words. "How long have you known?"

"Long enough."

Another long silence. "There are things you can take. Pills. Herbs. There are doctors in the city."

Even as these words left his mouth, she could not bring herself to believe he meant what he said. She'd never known such scandal. Who was this so-called man? How could she have so badly misjudged his character? The Lord had blessed her with the life that grew inside her—pure beauty—the life they had created together. What better way to bridge the two families than a child borne of love?

"Never speak of such things again. Our child's soul belongs to God and God alone."

"Agatha, please listen to reason. You must forgive me. We cannot stay here. They will never let us be together. Our only hope is to begin anew someplace else." He tossed his cigarette to the ground, reached out, and held her once more. His hands were like ice against her skin. "Please, my love. Leave with me. I will marry you. I promise to take care of you and our child."

And yet how could she believe him? How could she trust him after what he'd just said?

"Tell me how, Nathaniel. Where will we stay? What will you do for work?"

He released her and turned away. "You can't do this to me, Agatha. You'll ruin me. Can't you see that?" And then, seeing she was steadfast in her decision, he changed his tone. "That's it then. You've given me no choice."

He retreated to the shadows from which he'd emerged, leaving her with only the sting of his words. How could things have gone so wrong? All that time, all those months she'd spent with

Nathaniel, meeting him in out-of-the-way places, stealing kisses, and Agatha had nothing but love in her heart. What did she have now? What had she been left with?

A low wind blew over the field as she returned to the darkened house, chilling the panicked sweat on her bare skin. Back in her bed, beneath the heavy blankets, she tried in vain to warm herself, to cease her infernal shivering.

She repeated her prayers until dawn broke over the horizon, filling her world once more with the light and warmth of God. With it, her belief in goodness was restored. If the world was a void, she believed she could lend it form through the force of her love. She believed that Nathaniel would find it in his heart to do the right thing and that she would find it in hers to forgive him his misgivings. And in so doing, they would make the world a better place together.

So the days passed as they always had and as they always would, each giving way to the next, forming weeks, and then an entire, agonizing month. Agatha felt the life inside her taking shape, growing larger. Some mornings, she lay in bed and ran her hands over her belly, reciting her favorite names. Mary, Sarah, Rebecca, Ada, or Helen if she was a girl. James, Joseph, Daniel, Abraham, or August if he was a boy. Those moments filled her with profound joy and contentment. It was as powerful as an illness, euphoric, the world sent reeling, a fullness on the cusp of spilling over. Yet, this feeling would inevitably give way to an emptiness, the excruciating pain of knowing something was missing, that something, some integral part of her, was hidden away.

Each day she waited for Nathaniel to call, and each day she was disappointed when he did not. She knew she could not wait forever. For nearly a week now she had started to show, the small bump hidden easily enough by her wide dresses. Each passing day made informing her parents of her condition that much more difficult, that much more impossible.

And so she prayed. Nothing was impossible with God, though he moved in mysterious ways. This world was His kingdom. He planted his footsteps in the sea and rode upon the storm. Mountains rose from nothingness while ancient civilizations crumbled to sand and dust.

So it was, and so shall it be. One life begins and another ends.

One black morning at the tail end of summer, Agatha's grandmother quietly left this world behind. She was found in her bed by Agatha's mother, whose cries woke the house. The family doctor, a man named Bennet, paid a call later that day.

The old woman appeared to have died in her sleep, Bennet explained, and therefore without pain. A stroke, most likely. He sipped at his tea, the lenses of his gold-rimmed glasses steaming over.

Jeremiah held his wife as she wept, her body convulsing soundlessly. The boys sat next to each other on the floor, quiet and glum, resting their faces in their hands. The parlor wall clock ticked away heavy seconds. No one knew what to say. Agatha clasped her hands together, remembering the touch of her grandmother's skin. There were no words. There was only feeling, raw and untamed. Finally, the doctor set down his saucer and announced he had an appointment in town. He stood, offered his condolences, and shuffled out of the room.

Agatha followed. Bennet retrieved his coat from the hall stand, slid one arm through the coat's sleeve, turning slightly, and saw her standing there in the half-light, so utterly forlorn. God only knew what horrid look of shame she wore on her face. He offered a kind, knowing smile. "How long, my dear?"

With her mother's sobbing growing steadily more insistent from the next room, Agatha answered the doctor's question. He nodded as he finished putting on his coat, now reaching for his hat.

"And the child's father?"

Agatha shook her head. "We are married in the eyes of God."

"Indeed." Bennet paused for a moment, thinking. "Your father is a good and honorable man. A pillar of this community." He smiled once more, flashing a hint of tobacco-stained teeth. "See me in town as soon as you are able."

Jeremiah stepped into the hall and Agatha stiffened. She prayed that he would not see her in such a state, that he would not ask what the matter was. He drew close. She felt the weight of his hand fall upon her shoulder. "Is everything all right, Doctor?"

"Of course, Jeremiah. Agatha was merely seeing me out." And then, "She cries for her loss. Quite something, isn't she? A young woman of both charm and virtue."

Etiquette required a period of deep mourning to follow. Agatha's father was to wear a black suit and a black hatband, even at home, while her and her mother's dresses were trimmed with black crape. Velvet, satin, and lace were forbidden. All jewelry had to be removed. For the life of her, Agatha couldn't understand why such formalities were necessary. It seemed like a holdover from an older world, one of gloom and hopelessness, a bygone time when worship was drowned in darkness. It was out of step with the optimism she felt bubbling over in the outside world, the ceaseless outpouring of love she felt swelling in her heart each morning. She wanted more than anything to stay in the light, to be in the light, to feel His warmth, and be saved by it. Please, God.

She wanted so badly to remain strong for her little one, to feel loved and to pass down love like mothers do, like mothers should. But she couldn't fight it. The struggle was so tiring. She felt her world sliding away from her, down into the depths—

And found herself within a strange, darkened room. Her ragged breathing quickened. She flailed, felt smooth cold stone with one hand, then the other. Everywhere she touched she found cold, hard surface, closing in. A flat surface pushed against her back and the narrow panels of a coffin snapped into place. She tried to scream, only for clumps of dirt to fill her mouth. She choked on it. She couldn't move her arms, her legs. She was trapped. She was choking, submerged in silence as thick and cold as clay. And then she heard the sound of a shovel biting into the earth, somewhere up above, the sound of rocks and soil flung free, clattering against the lid of her coffin. She cried out. Why couldn't anyone hear her? Why weren't they helping her? Again and again, she heard these sounds, quieter upon each return, quieter still. The thought opened up inside her mind like a vacuous hole, sucking in the light: she had found her place in the world. She felt the light draining. From inside the light, she slid headlong into the dark, deep below the surface—forgotten. A candle snuffed out by the wind. She floated in outer space, fetal, turning slowly. The sound of her heartbeat filled the limitless void, joined now by another, softer, weaker. She heard the heartbeat of her unborn child, glowing red, in rhythm with her own, softer still, phasing, and then—

Someone pounded on the front door of House Underhill, insistent, angry. Agatha shot up in bed, blood pumping in her throat, arms and chest slick with sweat. She was nauseated, nearly threw up, interrupted only by another burst of rapping from downstairs, louder now. Her hands instinctively went to her stomach. Pale orange light flickered against her bedroom ceiling, liquid-rippled flame. It had been hellishly warm that night, and she'd slept with the window open. She went to it, looked out below, and saw the dark shapes of perhaps a dozen men gathered in the yard. They carried cloth-wrapped torches, the bright flames whipping in the wind.

Had there been an accident? A third burst of rapping rattled through the quiet house. Her heart pounded, breath heaving. Her father thumped down the stairs, cursing loudly, and threw open the front door. "What in God's name?"

"You know what this is about, Jeremiah." It was Silas, the mine foreman, a man welcomed into the Underhill's home countless times, who often joined the family for supper, who sat behind them in church. He was a man her father trusted, a gentle spirit with large, hard hands and a reddened baby-fat face. Until tonight, she'd never heard him so much as raise his voice. "You can't just shut down the mine as it suits you. The men need to work. You either give me the keys for the locks or you give the men half pay for their time off."

Agatha vaguely remembered her father explaining to her mother that operations at the mines were to stop, sometime soon after her grandmother had passed, she couldn't remember when, vaguely remembered overhearing something. It was only temporary, he said. He said it was out of respect for the dead.

Her father said something she couldn't hear. There was more back and forth and then Silas was yelling, practically pleading. "That's not the issue here, Jeremiah. These men won't be able to feed their families. Look inside your heart. They already pay you room and board out of the money you give them. Lord knows it isn't nearly enough."

"I'll ask you to watch your tongue and to leave the Lord out of this. The men are paid fairly. That's right. All of you. Maybe you should try spending less on drink and women."

There was more shouting, sharper than before, so much angrier than before. Something thumped against the side of the house—Agatha jumped—had someone thrown a stone?

"That's enough. I'm only here to deliver a message, Jeremiah. You should know that we've been meeting with Ephraim Bowles. We've listened to what he has to say. He makes a lot of sense. I'm telling you this as your friend, Jeremiah. You need to do better. You need to let your men work."

"I don't need to do anything of the sort. If the men are unhappy they can find work elsewhere. Bowles can open a mine of his own. And you can be the first to work for him, seeing as you no longer work for me."

He slammed the door. Agatha heard him stomp back up the stairs, then slam the door to the master bedroom. She heard her mother's voice, her frantic questions, her hysteria, and she heard her father silence her with a single barked command. Agatha turned her attention back to the yard. The men had started to disperse, grumbling among themselves. The light flickering across her ceiling faded to cool shadow, the flames of torchlight small as fireflies before they were swallowed by the night.

It was dark. And soon enough the darkness was replaced by the first light of morning. The events of the previous night were quickly forgotten, and with them any semblance of the known world.

From that day forward, everything changed. Whatever joy Agatha Underhill had known in her brief life—her memories of laughter and dancing, the sound of wind through the trees, the colored sunlight through a stained-glass window—all of it dissipated as she woke into a reality of unfamiliar and dangerous dimension.

No one knew what happened, not exactly. All they knew was that, just before dawn, Underhill's largest mine collapsed. The main entry was completely blocked off. Later, Agatha learned that Ephraim Bowles spread rumors that the collapse was the result of poor working conditions. He said there had been complaints of rotting box cribs, careless expansion, poisonous gases, dust explosions—anything you could think of. The abutment was too heavy. The beams were too weak. Others, those perhaps more loyal to Jeremiah Underhill, those with a stake in the town's prosperity, claimed they'd heard an explosion in the night. There was talk that Bowles had recently purchased dynamite, though no one could prove it.

Of course, Agatha didn't know any of that yet. That morning, all she knew was that something terrible had happened. And she could only believe that the responsibility lay with her and her alone, because that's exactly the kind of good and gentle soul she was. She was the kind of young woman who believed the world was a good place filled with good people who sought only to do the right thing—a person so incapable of knowing the evil in the hearts of men that she readily blamed herself for their misdeeds.

Jeremiah had locked himself in his office with some of his closest associates, shadowy men Agatha had seen only in passing, men whose names she did know, whose faces she did not recognize. They were men who did not belong to her family's church. She sat at the top of the stairs, a banister rail gripped tightly in each hand, something she used to do as a child when she listened to her parents argue late at night. Now, all these years later, she sat at the top of the stairs and she listened to these strange men argue about how something like this could have happened. She listened to them fight among themselves, laying blame, leveling accusations, and she felt just as helpless as she had all those years ago, a child cowering in fear.

And then she remembered Nathaniel's final words to her, out there in the yard, bathed in the clean light of the moon. She remembered him saying she'd left him no choice. She couldn't help but remember. Only now, this time, she recognized the tone of his voice for what it betrayed: anger, hatred, hurt.

Lord, she had been a fool to trust a Bowles. Please, Lord, forgive her for being such a fool.

Agatha waited for her father's associates to leave. And when they did, she went downstairs and stood before him, trembling. The cramped room smelled of sweat and stale smoke. Jeremiah looked up, surprised. She'd never once entered his office. For as long as she could remember, she had known it was a place where she did not belong.

She saw him there, her father—sitting behind his desk, looking oddly small, his shoulders slumped—and her heart broke for him. Everything she'd been given, and she'd thrown it all away. For what? For the dream of a man who had revealed himself to be a boy. Not even a boy, a snake.

The very thought of it brought tears to her eyes. She broke down. It was all too much. Jeremiah rushed to her and held her, told her everything would be all right. She didn't need to be scared, he said. There was an accident at one of the mines, that's all. It was just an accident. There was nothing to worry about.

"You don't understand. I know what really happened—and it's all my fault. I mean, it's them—the Bowles. But I brought it down upon us. They are getting back at both of us."

"What on Earth are you talking about, child?"

All the guilt, the shame, the feelings of foolishness and frustration, everything was suddenly on top of her, holding her down. She was still a child sitting at the top of the stairs. She'd gone out into the world too early. Her hands went to her stomach as she confessed to her father that she was pregnant. And her eyes dropped to the floor when she said the father was Nathaniel Bowles.

She never saw the slap coming, only felt it—her father's hard, open hand connecting with her cheekbone. She fell against the chair and would have fallen to the floor had he not grabbed whole fistfuls of her hair, yanking her out the door of his office and into the living room. She screamed then, once she knew what was happening, once the pain bloomed. Her hip slammed into a side table. She tried to find her footing, cried out. Her mother rushed from the kitchen, yelling. What in God's name? Jeremiah, what are you doing? What has she done?

Jeremiah ignored his wife, ignored his daughter's cries for mercy, for forgiveness. He rained down blows indiscriminately, on her head, her chest, her shoulders. She threw up her hands to protect herself, covering her face, the back of her head and neck, but he bent back her fingers until she screamed, until she let go. She tried to bite him and he punched her jaw. He kicked open the front door, grabbed her by the wrist and yanked so hard she heard her shoulder pop. The pain was everywhere. It took her breath away. He shoved her so hard she tumbled down the front steps, splayed out in the dirt below.

Agatha tasted blood. Her vision was rimmed red, pulsing. She picked herself up, her arms and legs shaking, her thigh throbbing, and saw her mother standing in the doorway, darkened by shadow. She was flanked by her brothers, both clutching at her aprons. They shouldn't have to see this, she thought. It wasn't fair to them. And then her father was on her again, commanding her to get up, to get moving, to quit her whimpering.

He marched her into town like she was cattle, shoving her, berating her. She was so overwhelmed, so surprised—so terribly relieved to have finally shed her dark secret—that she actually thought he was taking her to see Bennet. Instead, he took her to the sheriff, made her stand there, blood drying on her upper lip, and repeat what she'd said about Nathaniel Bowles, made her describe why she believed the Bowles had sabotaged the mine, how Nathaniel had threatened her and her family. And for his part, the sheriff listened quietly, impassively, leaning back in his chair with his boots up on his desk, crossed at the ankle. His jaw slowly rolled as he worked a wad of tobacco.

Finally, the sheriff had heard enough, waving his hand. He dropped his boots to the floor and leaned forward in his chair so they knew he meant what he said. There was nothing he could do, he said. Whatever proof might exist was buried down in the dust and the rubble of the collapse. He would not bring in Bowles for questioning. He turned his head and spit, dinging the spittoon on the floor. Do you think I wouldn't know if someone got their hands on dynamite? I know everything that happens in this town. And from what I can tell, he said, his lips glistening with tobacco juice, it seems like a straightforward case of structural collapse.

Jeremiah stood right there in front of God and everybody, looked the sheriff in the eye, and swore to take justice into his own hands. Agatha watched him, her hand pressed against her swollen jaw, prodding a loose tooth with her tongue, and prayed that he'd burst into flame.

After that, she was always alone, kept to her room, forbidden from being seen until the child was delivered—they only referred to it as such because it wasn't allowed a name—until the child could be given away. Her father ignored her. She may as well have been invisible.

During the long nights, there was only the Moon to keep her company, icy and indifferent. There was always the Moon. She saw it for what it was. A purifying light that hid a crawling darkness. She saw how the light blinded those who sought to look beyond, to the spaces between the stars. She saw how love was an illusion, how the light of the Lord was deceitful. There was only the infinite void of the world, the swimming black, endless, formless, and always so, so hungry.

She held the Moon's gaze each night, found her strength in its light. She closed her eyes and bowed her head and swore woe to all who betrayed her. And with her eyes closed, she allowed the darkness in, she chose the darkness, she let it take her.

Agatha woke to find the house empty. She called out and no

one answered. In the distance, she heard an open gate clapping in the wind.

She went downstairs and out into the yard to breathe in the fresh air. The sky was weirdly still. The leaves had changed color. Soon it would be wintertime. She went to the tree line and held a single, brittle leaf between two fingers. It made her want to cry.

There, from across the yard, she saw a man wearing a black cloth over his mouth walking toward her. His face and hands were stained with coal dust. He clutched a knife with a long blade at his side. He came to her slowly, as if walking through water. Agatha turned to flee, her movements equally slow, sluggish, and saw another man behind her, only this one had a length of thin rope held taut between two hands.

She was seventeen years old then, a young woman, no longer a girl. She was old enough to be out in the world, all on her own, and with it, she was old enough to experience all the bad things that followed.

There was the life growing inside her. The way her grandmother's skin felt in the days leading up to her death. How all life was ultimately revealed as so fragile. How quickly a living thing could be drained of its warmth, of its light.

All over the world, there were towns just like this one, built on the banks of wild rivers. And Agatha couldn't help but wonder how rivers came to be. Somewhere, surely, water bubbled up from beneath the ground and cut lines through the land. Over time the riverbed flattened, rocks were smoothed. And then one day it was there as if it had always been there, a river roaring with all its strength. There was no stopping it then.

How was that possible? How did it happen? Where had she gone wrong?

A HOTEL ROOM BY THE HIGHWAY

Lettie had been talking uninterrupted for some time. With the room's blackout curtains pulled tight, there was no telling how long exactly.

The hum of electricity filled the air. Lettie took a sip of water. Agatha's story had taken so much out of her, so much energy, so much emotion. She didn't have much left to give.

Barbara sat up straight in her chair, as composed and presentable as ever. She uncrossed and recrossed her legs. "What happened to Agatha Underhill?"

Lettie shrugged. "She went missing. That's as much as I know. They never found her again."

"And what does all this have to do with Courtney Bowles?"

Must she spell everything out so explicitly?

"Isn't it obvious? The disappearance of Agatha Underhill was where it all began. The bad blood. The curse. Whatever you want to call it. Agatha and Nathaniel's unborn child was innocent. It was pure. The death of the child was like a cancer. Something malignant. That malignancy grew and it swallowed everything good and then it grew some more."

"And killing Courtney Bowles was a means of—" Barbara searched for the right words. "Eliminating the cancer?"

"No, that's not quite—"

"Restoring balance?"

"Yes, that's right. That's exactly right. It was righting a wrong. That's why I did what I did." Lettie paused. "It wasn't easy. I knew I was throwing my life away, but I thought I was doing the right thing. I was doing it for all the right reasons. That's what I want people to know. I thought it would protect what was left of my family, maybe even secure the legacy of those who hadn't been born yet. And I thought it was what Courtney—Mrs. Bowles— wanted." Another pause. "I was so confused, so distraught. I mean, I still hadn't even gotten over Orn's death. And then I heard those nurses say that Mrs. Bowles had tried to kill herself. I couldn't believe it. Something inside me just snapped."

Lettie remembered the moment she removed the pillow from behind Court's head. She remembered looking into Court's eyes, seeing that she understood. Lettie placed her hand on Court's wrist, which was tied to the bed rail.

Court knew what needed to be done. She understood. Even if nobody else ever would, Court knew what Lettie had to do— and she was okay with it. She gave her permission.

"Somehow," Lettie said, "it made sense to give Mrs. Bowles what she wanted. In my own screwed-up way, I thought of it as an act of love. A gift."

"And what do you think now? Do you still believe you did the right thing?"

This was the big question. This was everything they had been working toward. Lettie knew what she was supposed to say. She knew what people wanted to hear. They wanted her to show remorse, be penitent, and receive redemption. That was how it was supposed to end. Full closure. Everything tied up with a bow. It would let everyone off the hook for their perverse interest. They wanted to believe that all this violence had culminated in the desperate act of a scared, deluded, drugged-up little girl.

But nothing was ever that simple. Given enough time, everything that happened between the two families, every action, had an equal and opposite reaction. Every fire extinguished sparked elsewhere. Every bullet that entered flesh exited somewhere else. And always the ground on which these events transpired had an unquenchable thirst for annihilation.

After Agatha disappeared, Jeremiah Underhill grew very rich. Ephraim Bowles went on to become sheriff, with Nathaniel serving as his deputy. Agatha's mother's hair went white. She went catatonic. Her brothers grew up to become unpleasant, angry young men.

One night, after years of believing the Bowles responsible for the abduction of their sister, Agatha's brothers broke into the Bowles's home. One of them blew the top of Ephraim's head off with a hammerless shotgun. The other one stabbed the sheriff's wife 32 times before slitting her throat. The four younger children were then killed one by one. One was found bound to his bed. Two others in the basement. And the fourth was found in the woods nearby, hunted down and butchered. When it was all over, Agatha's brothers set fire to the home, nearly burning it to the ground.

No one knew what happened to Nathaniel that night. It can only be assumed he safely escaped.

Agatha's brothers were found hiding in the woods a few weeks later. Both were half-starved and exhausted. Both were pelted with stones and publicly hanged. Their bodies remained strung up in the town square for several days, their purple, swollen faces picked clean by ravens and crows.

No, nothing was ever over, not between the two families. Not with the curse alive and well. By then, both sides had cousins living in town. Both families were quickly growing in number. And a series of violent altercations began to increase in both intensity and frequency.

Lettie looked Barbara in the eye. "I'm sorry—this is really hard."

"That's fine. You've been very brave, Letitia. I'll rephrase the question. Now that you've served your time and been released, do you believe that the curse has come to an end?"

Lettie remembered running her fingers over the carving in the wall of the stone chamber: A + N within the shape of a heart. She remembered the multitude of feelings it gave her, warmth and passion and pity and hatred. All that acid pumping through her blood. She'd been overwhelmed with the knowing.

Here she stood at the mouth of the abyss, knowing she must throw herself over its precipice. Even so, it did not anger her half as much as having to feign gratitude for doing so.

"Yes, I believe it's over. I'm so incredibly sorry for everything I've done and for everyone I've hurt. I learned so much about myself when I was in prison. I now see how messed up I was, how much I bought into the stories I'd heard about my family. These days, I believe only in the power of God's love. Nothing else. I believe that life is good and God is great."

She didn't hear much of what Barbara said after that—overwhelmed by the rush of fury, the crackling hum of electricity. The lights surged and her vision dimmed. She'd done what needed to be done, and now it was over. Once again, she heard the jarring, deep echo of a flipped industrial fuse switch, and a rush of cold darkness swept through the room.

Everything seemed to shift, a version of reality detaching from the original, sliding away. And when Lettie stood to leave, she felt as if she were leaving a version of herself behind, as if a version of herself would go on living in this room forever.

A few moments later, Lettie stood next to her small rented car in the hotel parking lot. A single sodium lamppost flickered nearby. It was freezing and she couldn't stop shivering. Snow fell in soft, wet clumps. The Moon shone above, an icy disc occasionally shrouded by purple and blue clouds. She lit a cigarette, her hand shaking. Then she closed her eyes and concentrated. By the time her cigarette had burned to its filter, she heard Mark's boots crunching against the slushy concrete.

He came to her then, standing a full head taller than her. His hands were stuffed in the pockets of his black peacoat.

"I was hoping I'd get a chance to talk to you again. I just wanted to tell you how great you were." He swallowed, licked his lips. He looked at her as if hypnotized. His voice went soft. "If you don't mind my saying so, I thought you were amazing. I mean, I think you are amazing."

"Thank you." She touched him on the elbow.

He couldn't help but smile.

Lettie allowed the warmth in her heart to pass through her, to become a part of him. And in return, she felt his heart open for her.

LETITIA UNDERHILL, THE WORLD BELOW

It took having a child of her own to learn what it meant to be a mother, what it meant to love and to pass down love, to be bonded by blood. It took the birth of her daughter—Stephanie Selene Underhill, her beautiful baby girl—to understand what it meant to be a protector of what is pure and good.

It's women who shed parts of themselves to form new life. A mother and her daughter, an act of irreparable violence, the baby ripped free of the womb, two things borne of one.

Men lack the strength. They lack the humility—the power of vision. They believe themselves to be in control because they have no other choice. The alternative—realizing they are obsolete, a means to an end—would be too much to bear. Look at those unfortunate moments in history when men wielded undue influence. Look at how they allowed a pervading fear of the unknown to justify barbaric acts of violence. Who did they persecute? Who did they blame for their impotence?

Women. It's always been women.

For nearly two years Lettie lived the life of a normal person.

She moved in with Mark, sharing his cramped one-bedroom apartment. He was good to her. He doted on her. He even cut himself off from his family after his parents voiced their disapproval.

Lettie got a job in a call center where she was able to make a living with minimal risk of being recognized. Her coworkers learned not to bother her. They learned to keep to themselves. She drove to and from work each day, sometimes stopping at a Starbucks drive-through on her way home. She learned to cook, she learned to bake, and she spent her evenings watching TV dramas about families who stuck together no matter what obstacles life threw their way.

She passed the long, lonely nights hunched in front of an old desktop computer, bathed in its harsh blue light, the only sounds Mark's softly snoring in the next room, the clicking of the keyboard. In those quiet moments, she felt an emptiness, a vacuous hole in place of her thoughts and feelings. She recalled the old house, and her memories opened up spaces within her, rooms without ceilings, without windows, discolored walls that stretched into an endless sky crawling with shadows.

The house continued on living inside her. She was still connected to it, could still feel its emptiness. She heard its strange sounds, those horrible moans of agony, and felt how its weight always seemed to be settling, seeking comforts hidden deeper in the earth.

And there—in that space, channeling that connection—she heard Stephen's voice calling to her across distant, fire-swept plains, as if picking up a radio signal from another world.

He was out there, her missing half. He was still alive.

She'd first heard his voice in prison. He came to her that morning the COs swept into her cell, three men wearing black latex gloves. She had only a moment to react—a few seconds, really—but she was fast, she was ready. She fished out the cellophane packet of ten strips she kept tucked into the top bunk's metal bed frame. She stuffed them into her mouth. Nobody noticed, or if they did, they didn't care. The COs made her stand in the hall with her hands on the wall. One of them patted her down as the other two tore apart her cell. They made a big show of searching through her stuff. They slashed her mattress with a box cutter. They rifled through her papers, fanned the pages of her books. They dumped out her toiletries, her commissary items. All along they knew exactly what they were looking for. One of them came out of the cell holding the small Visine bottle between his gloved thumb and forefinger, gave it a little shake. Look at what we have here. What do you think we'll find once we have this tested?

They took her down to the hole. White cinderblock walls. No mattress. No toilet. No running water. She didn't know how long she was down there. The acid kicked in hard. It felt like she'd been born there, like she would never leave, like she'd never been born at all, like she'd never left.

The walls, the floor, the ceiling were a single continuous surface, as perfect and fully formed as the shell of an egg. And she was trapped inside the egg, waiting to be reborn. She saw patterns of tiny black holes in the perfect white shell, breathing, hundreds, thousands, millions of tiny black holes.

She made herself tiny, squeezed down into one of those holes, and she tumbled into outer space, the planet flung away beneath her feet. It was so cold. Then she heard him. He called to her.

That was when Stephen first revealed himself to her, filled her with his presence like light born in darkness, everywhere and all at once.

He told her he had ascended and taken refuge among the stars, like smoke released into the night-time sky, and that he was sorry for leaving her alone. He told her that she would be free again. There was nothing to fear. I've always been here, he said. Someday soon I will tell you how to join me. Then he pulled back the veil of space and time, showed Lettie the source of all knowledge, an ocean of consciousness—a black-eyed fetus tucked tight in a blood-red fold.

"He'll wake soon. A new god."

And so years later, she sat there before the computer's sickly blue light and wrote down everything her brother told her. She listened as he told her everything she did not know. He showed her the night Orn disappeared, the events leading up to the House Underhill Massacre, the morning after the fire. He showed her everything, as he always had. She typed until the muscles in her forearms were tight and twisted, until her fingers ached, and the cold light of the outside world bled around the edges of the curtains.

One week after Lettie submitted the final manuscript to her agent, she discovered she was pregnant. Everything else quickly fell into place. The book went to auction and sold for an enormous amount of money, far more than Lettie, or anyone else, had ever expected. The film rights sold, foreign-language rights, audio— everything. The first payment on the advance was enough for Lettie to leave her job. Together, she and Mark made a down payment on an old house in a small town in Wisconsin, just past the Illinois border. And by the time the book was published, their daughter had entered the world, as beautiful and special as all the Underhill women who had come before her.

They were a family then, her and Mark and Stephanie. Everything was perfect. Or so it should have been. Lettie couldn't help but feel something was missing. There was nothing where there should have been something, an insatiable hole that drained away whatever joy she felt the moment she felt it, an inconsolable sadness always reminding her that this was not the way it was supposed to be. She did not deserve such happiness. She was cursed. Everything she knew was cursed. Everything she wanted was cursed. Everything she touched was cursed. Everything she ever cared about was cursed.

So she bided her time. If nothing else, her years in prison had taught her to be patient. Months passed. And then finally, late one night, as she lay in bed staring at the ceiling, Stephen's voice returned and revealed to her the final secret.

He showed her Jeremiah Underhill at his desk in his office, the door closed. The room was dark, lit by an oil lamp. Blades of warm, orange light slashed at the walls. He tipped a bottle of whiskey into a glass, poured out three fingers, and drained it in a single swallow. A painted portrait of his family hung on the wall across the room. Lettie saw the way Jeremiah admired his daughter's beauty, the way he tilted his head and smirked, how he took pride over her as one would a possession.

Then Jeremiah threw the empty whiskey glass at the wall, where it narrowly missed the painting and shattered. He buried his face in the crook of his arm, slumped over his desk, and wept.

Lettie saw how Bennet came to Jeremiah shortly after the funeral, how the doctor demanded payment to keep Agatha's pregnancy a secret. Jeremiah, he said, you're a wealthy man. Surely you wouldn't mind investing in our town's first hospital?

Surely you would be willing to convince the town council to have it named for me? That's not too steep a price to pay for the sake of your good name, is it?

She saw how Jeremiah paid two desperate transients in town to follow Bennet home the next night, to put a knife between his ribs, to make the whole thing look like a robbery gone wrong. She saw how Jeremiah instructed the men to have his own daughter abducted and killed, her body dumped in the depths of the coal mines, where no one would ever find it.

And so Jeremiah wept—not for Agatha, not for the loss of his daughter's life, her happiness, her future—but for the loss of his pride, for his humiliation, the sacrifice he had been forced to commit. He blamed Agatha and Agatha alone. A child borne of bad blood, an unholy union. How could he ever let such an abomination enter the world?

That was how it all began, the moment where it all went wrong. And now, all this time later, Lettie finally knew what she must do.

That night, after Mark had gone to sleep, Lettie took a knife from the kitchen and climbed the stairs. The house was dark, quiet. She wore her hair pulled back. She entered the bedroom she shared with her husband. Cold moonlight filled the large picture window.

Mark slept on his back and breathed through his mouth, his wide chest gently rising and falling, rising and falling. Lettie stood over him and watched him sleep. She listened to the sound of his breathing.

He was just as bad as all the others. How could something as beautiful as their daughter have come from something so ugly?

With a strength she did not think possible, Lettie thrust the tip of the blade into the base of Mark's chin, saw it slide through and into his open mouth, glinting in the moonlight, pricking his thrashing tongue. A slash of hot blood shot across her wrist. Mark's eyes opened. He tried to scream but couldn't move his mouth. He grabbed at Lettie's wrists, but she was too fast. She pulled free the blade and stuck him in his ribs, in his stomach, the side of his neck, his throat. He gurgled each time. She slashed at his hands, his face, wherever she could. He was sobbing then, pleading, his movements getting slower, weaker. The blade glided cleanly through his flesh, snagged on bone. Each strangely silent stroke flung blood all over the room, the bed, the headboard.

Finally, Mark stopped moving. Only a quivering mess remained. Lettie dropped the knife to the floor. Her hands shook. A moment later she realized she was laughing, and once her laughter died down, she heard Stephanie crying from her nursery.

Lettie took a shower and did her best to remove the bloodstains from her skin. Then she wrapped Stephanie in a blanket, calmed her down, and placed her in her car seat. Lettie drove long into the night. And in the early morning hours, they passed the old covered bridge over Copper Creek and returned to the woods she had once called home.

Lettie cradled Stephanie against her chest as she walked the familiar low valley between two hills, oak trees on one side, elm on the other. The first hints of sunlight bled the deep color from the sky, a long wrap of feverish yellow. Winds gently rustled the leaves overhead. She climbed the slope of old railroad ties, now nearly rotted away.

Where once House Underhill stood proud, there was now a field of tall grass. And though Lettie could not see the house, she knew it was still there. She knew the most important parts of it—the places that mattered most—were merely hidden from view.

She pulled free the boards over the entrance to the coal mine, the rusty nails squeaking as they slid through the rotted wood. Memory guided her way as she navigated the cold, dark tunnels, as she held Stephanie in one arm and dragged her free hand along the smooth stone walls. She trudged through cold, knee-deep water, crouched beneath the low ceilings, carefully threaded through the maze of pillars. Finally, she reached the room that still called to her all these years later.

She sat cross-legged in the center of the room, holding Stephanie tight. She kissed her sweet baby girl on her forehead and told her that no matter what happened she would always love her. This is something your mama has to do, she said. I know you'll understand.

The darkness in that room was complete, the kind of pitch black that existed only underground, beyond the reach of light. Lettie took it in. She let it fill her. The darkness became her, welcomed her. She opened herself to it. And in return, she saw a single eye there in its depths. Then another. Soon there were thousands, millions of eyes—as many as there were stars in the sky—each unblinking.

Stephen emerged from the black. He crawled out of an invisible hole—both impossibly close, impossibly far away—covered head to toe in a shimmering, tar-like substance. The light seemed to bend around his innumerable limbs, the insect-like rhythm of his gait. He was both the stars and the darkness. He was both everything and nothing, the one who strides across the curve of the black mirror.

He extended his arm to her, told her he had been waiting for her, suspended in the ooze from which all things are born and to which all things return. Come, he said, I will show you.

Still cradling her daughter against her breast, Lettie took Stephen's hand in hers. The child's cries traveled light-years through space, echoing across vast, empty plains. She placed her hand over her daughter's mouth, felt her go quiet. There was nothing to fear. They were a family again. The three of them shared the same blood.

Together, they ascended beneath the gaze of the giant floating eyeball at the center of all things. Together, they become whole. They formed a single being of eternal wisdom, undying vengeance, and pure innocence. And in this way, they would live forever as a family.

From the height of their ascension, they saw the beginning and the end. They saw how it bent back into a circle, the birth of the snake from its cosmic egg, forever chasing after its own tail. They saw how it coiled into itself, finding an inner strength. And from within the center of the eternal wheel, a vast and unknowable rage.

They saw Agatha Underhill drag her broken, bloodied legs behind her through the dark tunnels of the mine, her abductors having neglected to check her pulse. And they saw her spend her final moments using a sharp stone to carve something into the wall. After all, people always finds things to believe in when they're trapped, when they're dying. They can't help but hold onto things to believe in, a vision of a better world, a more just life.

A tiny pinprick of light bloomed there in the dark. Slowly it grew larger, until it took the shape of a room. And within that room, looking so much older now, Scud Bowles sat in an armchair watching TV. He looked so much like his dad, Franklyn. And he shared so many of the same weaknesses. He drank too much. He picked fights with his wife, wore down her resistance. He bullied his own children, took out his anger on those around him, those who were smaller than him, weaker, unable to protect themselves.

Scud picked up the remote and turned off the TV. The room was quiet then. He idly wondered where his wife had taken the kids. It seemed like he was always alone these days. He sighed and got out of the chair. Maybe they didn't want him to find them.

He opened the door in the kitchen and descended the staircase to the basement. There, he knelt before the cabinet-sized gun safe, and typed the code into the keypad—the six digits of Orn's birthday.

Could he really blame them? Could he really hold it against the people in his life for wanting to avoid him?

He removed the most powerful gun he owned, a .44 magnum.

Many times over the years, Scud had wondered about the last night of Orn's life. Many times, he had asked himself what the hours and minutes leading up to his brother's death must have felt like. What had he seen? What had he felt? Had he known he was going to die alone?

Scud placed the barrel of the gun beneath his chin. His finger curled around the trigger. The hammer pulled back ever so slightly.

His face relaxed. He closed his eyes.

Would anyone be there waiting for him on the other side?

Would they forgive him?

He liked to think so.

David Peak's books include *Eyes in the Dust and Other Stories* (Trepidatio Publishing), *Corpsepaint* (Word Horde), and *The Spectacle of the Void* (Schism). He lives in Chicago.

www.ingramcontent.com/pod-product-compliance
Lightning Source LLC
Chambersburg PA
CBHW030635190726

48286CB00008B/2533